"I'll find a judge who isn't tied to the Powers purse strings."

Matthew scoff█████████████████████ You forget, I'm not █████████████████████ state investiga█████████████████████ state of Arkans█████████████████████ne judge they don't█████████

"Good luck."

"As a matter of fact, I already have a couple in mind. And I bet if you stop letting them get into your head, you can probably come up with other possibilities."

"They aren't in my head."

"They are. You're as awed by them as Mallory was, but in a different way. Don't let the flash and bluster blind you. That guy is scared. Scared enough to assemble his own dream team to take a simple meeting with a lowly detective from the state police."

"I doubt he goes anywhere without an entourage."

"Right. And when there's a crowd, there's bound to be a witness. It's only a matter of watching and waiting."

"You already have a mark."

She nodded. "Yep."

OZARKS MISSING PERSON

MAGGIE WELLS

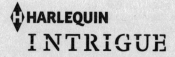

HARLEQUIN
INTRIGUE

Thank you, Brinda, Kelli and Megan, as well as all my true
crime addicts, for playing endless games of what-if with me.
Sometimes truth really is stranger than fiction.

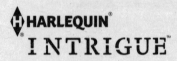

Recycling programs
for this product may
not exist in your area.

ISBN-13: 978-1-335-58262-1

Ozarks Missing Person

Copyright © 2023 by Margaret Ethridge

For questions and comments about the quality of this book,
please contact us at CustomerService@Harlequin.com.

Harlequin Enterprises ULC
22 Adelaide St. West, 41st Floor
Toronto, Ontario M5H 4E3, Canada
www.Harlequin.com

Printed in U.S.A.

By day **Maggie Wells** is buried in spreadsheets. At night she pens tales of intrigue and people tangling up the sheets. She has a weakness for hot heroes and happy endings. She is the product of a charming rogue and a shameless flirt, and you only have to scratch the surface of this mild-mannered married lady to find a naughty streak a mile wide.

Visit the Author Profile page at Harlequin.com.

CAST OF CHARACTERS

Grace Reed—Special agent of the Arkansas State Police Criminal Investigation Division. A specialist in seeking out missing persons, she's on a mission to find a young woman named Mallory Murray, who failed to come home from work one night.

Matthew Murray—Mallory's estranged brother and Benton County assistant DA. Alerted to his sister's disappearance, Matthew is determined to make amends by finding out what happened to the younger sister he barely knew.

Mallory Murray—A local woman with an eye on climbing the social ladder. When Mallory's body is found floating in Table Rock Lake, the police are immediately suspicious of her connection to local playboy Trey Powers.

Tyrone (Trey) Powers III—The handsome but entitled scion of a prominent and highly connected dynasty of politicians and attorneys, Trey believes he's above the law because his family makes the laws.

Harold Dennis—The Powers family's personal attorney, and the biggest obstacle standing between Grace and Matthew and the truth.

Prologue

Mallory Murray tipped her chin up and stared at the velvety black of the midnight sky. She would swear it was a shade darker on this tiny inlet of Table Rock Lake than anywhere else. The stars gleamed bright white against the backdrop. Thousands of them spread out like polka dots.

Beneath her feet, a powerful engine revved. The sleek boat knocked against the floating dock as Trey and another guy threw off the lines and hauled in the bumpers. Instinctively, she widened her stance to keep her balance. She was born on these lakes. Had been boating since she could walk. But her dad's ancient pontoon was nothing like the expensive ski boat she stood on now.

And she wasn't a carefree young girl excited to go swimming. She had a larger mission at hand. One she wasn't certain she could accomplish. The food she'd consumed since arriving at the Powerses' lake house threatened to come back up, but she closed her eyes and forced herself to breathe evenly. She had to focus.

Though she had grown up less than fifteen miles from the spot where Trey Powers's grandfather had built his eccentric but spectacular castle in the Ozark wilderness, it may as well have been a different galaxy. The locals and the wealthy families who established their weekend escapes on waterfront parcels didn't often mix. Their mutually beneficial relationship was cordial but nowhere near friendly. People like Mallory and sweet Mrs. Gibbons, the housekeeper Trey's family employed, were usually working in more of a service capacity. The lake people rarely mixed with locals socially.

Except for Mallory and Trey. She and Trey Powers had been *interacting* for nearly five years, off and on. Now, she was ready to flip the switch to on. Permanently.

"Everybody ready?" Trey called from his spot behind the wheel.

The night breeze blew her hair into her face as she turned, but Mallory didn't care. She aimed her brightest, widest smile on him, afraid if she tried to shout over the roar of the engine a quaver in her voice might give her away.

Trey grinned as a chorus of cheers rose from the four other passengers crammed onto the back of the boat. An answering roar came from the crowd on the pontoon in the next slip.

Mallory cast a wary glance at the revelers on the other boat. There were too many of them on board. There certainly weren't enough life jackets to go around. And nearly everyone had been drinking. Possibly for hours. But rules and regulations didn't apply to Trey Powers.

His family made them for others to follow.

With his hand wrapped around the throttle, Trey jerked his chin, signaling for her to come closer. She complied.

The kiss he planted on her was hard and sloppy. She could taste the lingering smokiness from the scotch he'd been drinking on his lips and did her best not to cringe. Trey was handsome. He was the heir to his family's law firm in Bentonville. Over the years, Mallory had often wondered which had come first, the Powers name or the actual power the people born under it had accumulated.

Her heart thrummed along with the engine as he eased the throttle up. The boat bumped the slip when he backed out, and she ducked away from the towing bar, where racks of wakeboards wavered perilously close.

She'd been relieved to see him today. Not because she'd missed him, but because almost eight weeks had passed since they were together, and she'd had no way to contact him. Trey liked to make a joke out of not giving her his phone number, telling her she'd see him when she saw him. And he always came around. But now… Now, she needed to see him and hadn't wanted to try to reach him through his family's firm.

Moving closer to where Trey stood at the wheel, she tried to shout over the blaring music coming from the boat's state-of-the-art sound system. "Maybe we shouldn't go out."

But Trey couldn't hear her. Or chose not to. He and his friends had already been partying when they stumbled into Stubby's, the roadside bar and grill on Highway 62 where she worked.

He'd told her they were on their way from Beaver Lake to the Powers place on Table Rock Lake for a crawfish boil. It was clear they'd been drinking most of the day, but Trey was his usual charming, friendly self. His face lit when he walked through the door and spotted her. The last she'd seen of him was the back of his mussed hair as he exited the storeroom behind the bar where they'd hooked up. Again.

But he must have been genuinely pleased to see her, because he left the pouty girl he'd walked in with to invite her to come along to his family's place on the lake for the party. He'd never invited her to go farther than the back room. Or the parking lot.

Mallory had untied her apron as fast at her eager fingers would allow. Steve, the guy who owned Stubby's, made his customary threats about firing her, but she'd ditched out on shifts before. She knew Steve's threats were empty ones. Good waitresses weren't easy to come by out in the Middle of Nowhere, Arkansas. When she showed up for her shift Saturday night, they'd both act like nothing had happened.

Trey revved the boat's powerful engine, jolting her into the present. She backed off a step. A midnight cruise with Trey Powers by her side was too tempting to pass up. They'd been playing this game of cat and mouse since she was eighteen, sleeping together every now and again for the better part of those years. But he'd been around less frequently this summer, and she could sense him slipping through her fingers. Yesterday it had looked like she was running out of options, but today it felt like fate was smiling on her.

She'd never been inside anywhere near as fancy the legendary lake house built by the first Tyrone Delray Powers. She'd done her best not to gawk when he led her into the place. On the outside, it looked like some kind of European castle, but on the inside it was all luxurious hunting lodge, complete with gleaming wood beams, real wood paneling and dozens of taxidermic trophies dotting the walls.

She could totally see herself throwing parties there once she and Trey made things official.

Trey gave the engines a bit more juice, and the boat began to move. Psyching herself up to play the wild-child role she knew he expected from her, she called out, "Let's do this!" with far more enthusiasm than she felt.

Trey threw his head back and laughed. Mallory smiled to herself, proud she'd pleased him. He'd once told her he liked her because she made him laugh. She was fairly sure the easy laughter they shared was what kept him coming back.

Trying to be unobtrusive, she grasped the safety bar as he swung the boat wide. One of the other women aboard fell forward against the back of Mallory's seat, giggling and crying out a slurry "Whoops!"

Even in the dim light, Mallory could see the petite girl's brown hair had been meticulously, and probably expensively, highlighted to a warm tawny gold. She dug her French-tipped nails into the pristine white leather upholstery as she attempted to regain her balance.

Of course, Trey chose that moment to take off at full speed.

The bow of the boat lifted, and the other girl tumbled back into one of Trey's friends. He stood out from the usual gaggle of young fellow hotshot lawyers who followed Trey around like ducklings. He was older. Stiffer. And Mallory would swear he looked vaguely familiar. Like she'd seen his face on the news or a billboard or something.

She tightened her grip on the safety bar. A startled

laugh popped out of her as the front of the boat hit the water with a hard slap.

"Easy, cowboy," she called to Trey, but the wind ripped the words away.

Her hair streamed back from her face. Any minute now, Trey would turn against the night breeze and the loose strands would start whipping her mercilessly, but she didn't want to tie it back. She had to contain it every shift she worked at Stubby's. The wind sliding through it and lifting the weight of it from her shoulders felt glorious.

True to his reckless nature, Trey was driving too close to the shoreline for safety. As they zoomed past the shadowy figures of towering trees backlit by a sliver of moon, Mallory smirked. It was a good thing the Powers family and timber companies owned most of the adjoining acreage. There would be no neighbors to complain.

God, she loved this life. Deep down in her heart, she believed she was meant for it. She wanted it so badly she could taste it. And she was so close. All she had to do was convince Trey their future was written in the stars, and she'd have it all.

She wouldn't have to bust her hump working the way her brother did, scraping together every bit of prestige he could. No, she would have everything she'd ever wanted tied up in one big package with a silky white bow.

Trey eased up on the speed long enough to shout something back to one of his pals. A chorus of voices protested, but Trey ignored them.

Trey rarely did anything except exactly what he wanted to do.

But Mallory had always been able to key into Trey's moods. Tonight he was restless and rowdy. The crowd he'd started with at Stubby's had tripled in size when the caterers had dumped the food onto butcher paper–covered trestle tables. After they feasted, the serious drinking began.

Shots were poured and tossed back with abandon. Dares and taunts flew back and forth across the massive fire pit built into the terraced patio. She knew when Trey said something about taking the boat out for a cruise, he would make it happen. She also knew when he was in one of these moods, the best thing anyone could do was go along.

Giving in, she yanked the elastic hair band from her wrist and bundled her hair up in a messy bun atop her head.

"You okay over there, beautiful?" Trey asked her.

Beautiful. He always called her beautiful. Like her looks were the sum total of who she was. And, to Trey, they probably were. Sometimes she wondered if he even remembered her name. But it didn't matter. Soon, he'd never forget it.

"Everything's perfect," she replied.

In that moment, she meant it.

Mallory gazed upward again and stared at the infinite blanket of stars above them. She fixated on one in particular. It burned so brightly she wondered if it was actually an airplane winging its way across the night sky. She stood engrossed, forgetting to take hold of the bar again or plant her feet to brace against the boat's sudden acceleration.

A sharp round of squawks and squeals erupted behind her. Trey swung the wheel wide to the left, playing chicken with the shoreline. Mallory righted herself enough to make a grab for the top of the windscreen, but her first attempt missed. She grabbed hold as the silhouettes of the looming trees moved closer at an alarming rate. Trey's laughter drifted to her on the wind.

"You're not scared, are you, beautiful?" he mocked.

She shook her head and released her hold, stubbornly refusing to give him the satisfaction. With her feet under her again and her knees flexed, she forced another smile and wagged her head. "Nope."

To prove her point, she shifted her gaze from the rapidly approaching shore to the sky yet again, looking upward, pretending she hadn't a care in the world. It was a beautiful sight. One of those clear summer nights when the heavens felt close enough to touch.

Another guy aboard gave a shout. Trey laughed and turned the wheel sharply. The boat pitched to starboard. Mallory continued to stare at the sky, pleased she wasn't the one to flinch, even if her stomach was heaving. Trey would be happy. If she made Trey happy, maybe he would make her happy in return. She hoped.

The boat slowed to a sedate cruise, and she exhaled long and shaky, grateful she hadn't lost her dinner over the side.

"You okay there?" he asked, his voice low and intimate.

She was still looking up, a smug smile curving her lips. She should have waited to tell him there, out on the water. It would have been much better than blurting it in the kitchen. She could have plastered a dopey, smitten smile on her face and let the wind carry the words

I'm pregnant to him. Maybe he would have been more excited about it all.

Instead, he'd gone all lawyer on her. Asking all the questions she knew he would ask but hoped he wouldn't. It took all the restraint she could muster not to go off on him. She'd managed to nod and play it cool when he said they'd talk more about it in private.

She'd wait. See how he wanted to handle things. And if his answers weren't to her liking, maybe she'd see how his mama and daddy felt about having a grandbaby.

"I'm great," she answered, pressing her hand to her stomach as she leaned in to kiss his stubbled cheek. "Now get this sardine can moving."

"Yes, ma'am," he answered smartly and took up his position at the wheel once more.

There was a rev and a roar as the boat's turbocharged props kicked into gear. It was obnoxious, but she laughed out loud. The people behind them screeched, whooped and shouted. A cheer went up from the other boat as some of the guys lit Roman candles and fired them into the sky.

Trey slowed, allowing the others to turn and watch. A wakeboard someone hadn't secured to the rack slid across the decking as the boat rocked wildly in its own residual wake.

"Here, let me get this out from between us," Trey said, then he bent to scoop up the board. "Forgot to put it on the rack."

Out from between us. Soon there'd be nothing between them. Soon, he'd be all hers. She had to believe her dreams would come true.

Throwing her head back, she caught sight of a pink

fireball in the sky. She traced its arc as she let the day-dream take hold.

Trey Powers.

Mallory Powers.

Trey and Mallory Powers.

What would be a good nickname for sweet little Tyrone Delray Powers the Fourth? He had a cousin called Del. Maybe Chip?

She was tossing names around in her head when the deck shifted and Trey stepped closer. The change in momentum threw her. She heard the zip whistle of a bottle rocket zooming into the sky. The deck shifted again, and she reached up for the tow bar. A whisper of warm, whisky-scented breath tickled her cheek. She lowered her head to peer at Trey, but something hit her hard on the head. Distantly, she heard the *thunk* of it, but everything started to spin.

She was falling.

Fainting?

Someone shouted.

The chill of the water shocked her into stillness. Mallory caught one more glimpse of the twinkling stars.

Then everything went black.

Chapter One

Special Agent Grace Reed took a deep slug from the aluminum bottle she filled to the brim each morning. It made a loud clank as she placed it back on her desk, but she didn't tear her gaze from her computer. The screen was filled with the gap-toothed smile of five-year-old Treveon Robinson, a boy who disappeared while on a trip to the grocery store with his mom.

The case had kept her up all night. Missing children were automatically an instant cause of insomnia, but it wasn't only his disappearance bothering her. It was the knowledge there'd be no billboards or citywide awareness campaigns for Treveon.

Sure, there'd been a feature on the local news—a teary plea from his mama to send her baby home safely. They had issued an Amber alert, and phones all over Arkansas, Texas, Oklahoma and Missouri had buzzed. But the cold, hard truth of the matter was kids named Treveon didn't get the same attention from the media, and therefore the public, as kids named Cody or Tyler or Justin.

Could the worth of one boy be measured in a string of random letters used to form a name? A name Patricia

Robinson said she'd chosen because her baby deserved a name as unique as he was.

The photograph had captured a mischievous gleam in the boy's dark eyes. He looked like an angel, but according to the stories his mother and grandmother had shared, he had a bit of the devil in him.

If she couldn't catch a break on his disappearance soon, she would have to turn his case over to McAvoy in the Crimes Against Children division. Staring into those eyes now, Grace swore to herself she would not forget Treveon.

Of course, she would continue the hunt for Treveon long after the news cycle dropped him into a bucket of sad statistics.

"Hey, Reed, I have another MP for you," the agent assigned to desk duty, Jim Thompson, called to her, waggling a phone receiver above his head.

And, of course, he was sending the missing person call to her. The guys always funneled them her way. Not because she was particularly good at solving the cases, but because they were too often addicts who'd gone on a bender, or spouses who'd decided to pack up and go. In short, the other agents couldn't be bothered.

There wasn't a lot of turnover in the Arkansas State Police Criminal Investigation Division. Particularly in Company D, based in her hometown of Fort Smith. Even after three years here, and five more in Little Rock, she was still one of the lower-ranking agents on the team.

Therefore, she drew the short straw when it came to catching cases and had unofficially become Miss Missing Persons to the rest of the guys. Not a job she'd ever aspired to hold. Like most ambitious detectives, Grace wanted to sink her teeth into some of the more high-profile cases.

But she was patient. The bigger cases would come. For now, she would keep searching for those most people forgot about the minute the news cycle moved on and the posters grew faded.

She glowered at the blinking red light indicating a call was holding for her and snatched up the receiver. "CID, Agent Reed speaking," she said briskly.

"Agent Reed? Brett Baines, Carroll County Sheriff's Department. I guess you're the go-to lady to talk to when it comes to girls who don't come home."

Grace recognized the deep male voice on the other end of the line. She and Baines had worked a previous case together. Closing her eyes, she sent up a silent prayer this case might end better than the last one had. "Deputy Baines,. How can I help you?"

"I got a call a while ago from a young lady named Kelli Simon. She tells me her roommate hasn't been home in days." He paused, letting the information sink in. "I get the impression from talking to her this isn't unusual behavior on the part of the roommate, but the electric bill is due, and the missing girl hasn't paid her part… Probably went up to Branson and blew it all on a purse or something."

He chuckled and Grace bristled. Bitingher lip to keep from biting his head off for that coming she plucked a pen from a coffee cup with the state police logo on it and pulled the notebook she kept on her desk closer. She scribbled, *electric bill due*, asking, "What was the name again?"

"Reported by Kelli Simon—"

"Kelly with a *Y*?" she asked.

"An *I*. Apparently, Kelli with an *I* called her room-mate's place of employment to track her down and found out she hasn't been in to work, either."

"The missing woman's name?" Grace prompted.

"Murray. She's called Mallory Murray," Deputy Baines said, enunciating each syllable of the missing woman's name. "She's twenty-three years old, single, Caucasian, dark brown hair and blue eyes. Last seen at work on Friday evening."

Today was Tuesday. More than three days had passed, Grace noted as she added the details to her notes.

"And they're roommates?" she asked. "House? Apartment?"

"They rent a place here in Eureka. Apartment, I think," he said, seemingly looking back through his own notes.

Grace scribbled *Eureka Springs* at the top of the page. "Did she have any guesses as to a height or weight?"

"Miss Simon said maybe about five-six or-seven. She said she was a few inches taller than her and she's five-four. As for a weight, she only said skinny." He chuckled. "Not much help, I know. I have a daughter who's about that age, and *skinny* is a relative term to some young ladies."

Deputy Baines said the last with a hefty dose of good-old-boy bonhomie, but Grace was in no mood to play along. She could already envision the media cov-erage a pretty young white woman would garner, and while she knew every bit helped, she couldn't ignore the twinge of resentment she felt when her gaze strayed to Treveon's photo.

Dragging herself back, she forced herself to sit up straighter. Every citizen deserved her undivided attention. "Approximately five foot six or more and slim," she repeated, emphasizing the word *slim*.

"Yes, ma'am."

"I assume you're going to email me whatever information you have?" she asked.

"Yes, ma'am," the deputy repeated. He didn't sound sad to be handing this one off to the state police. "Ms. Simon said she was sending over some photos. I'll wait for those to come through and send it all to you at once."

Grace scowled at the notepad. How she wished she could clear these cases from her mind as easily as these guys moved them off their desks.

"I assume since you're passing this to me you gave the roommate…uh, Ms. Simon, my contact info?" Grace asked. She drew a line from her period up to the top of the page, making an arrow out of it, and began to print the name *Kelli*.

"I told her you'd reach out to her," the deputy informed her. "I wasn't sure how snowed under you were, and I thought that might be better."

Grace tapped the end of her pen against the notebook. "Sure. Fine."

"Her cell number is…" He rattled it off. "Probably should try texting her. If she's anything like my kids, she won't answer a phone call from an unknown number."

Grace rolled her eyes at the man's derision but acknowledged him. "I will."

"I'll have her email address and other pertinent information in the report, and if I hear anything more from her before you can make contact, I'll refer her directly to you." He paused for a moment. "If it's okay with you, of course."

In no mood for his feigned deference, Grace sat up straighter and removed the receiver from where she held it pinched between her shoulder and ear. "Absolutely okay with me. Might as well eliminate the middleman, right?" She tossed her pen down. "Good speaking to you, Deputy. I'll be looking for your report."

Grace placed the receiver in its cradle and blew out a long breath. Leaning back in her chair, she tipped her chin to the ceiling and focused on the breathing exercises her bohemian sister, Faith, had insisted she learn.

Inhale, exhale. Inhale, hold, exhale.

She forced herself to repeat the exercise over and over. Whether it helped or not, she couldn't say, but it sure didn't hurt when it came to dealing with men like Baines. You'd think after spending her entire career letting their ingrained misogyny roll off her back, she'd be impervious to microaggressions.

But she wasn't.

While she waited for the deputy to pass along the information, Grace clicked through the pages of the file she'd accumulated on young Treveon. Her stomach roiled, and without thinking she opened the center drawer of her desk and pulled out a roll of antacids. She popped two tablets into her mouth and chomped down hard. There were days when she wondered why she'd chosen this path, and this was one of them.

But in all honesty, most days she couldn't imagine herself doing anything else. From the age of twelve, all she'd wanted was to be a detective. She knew in her soul her destiny was to be an instrument of justice. After all, someone had to make sense of her mother's senseless death. And the job was clearly up to her.

Sitting straighter in her chair, she reminded herself she couldn't win them all. But maybe, just maybe, she'd win one or two here and there and in her own way help make somebody else's life more bearable. Glancing at the open notebook, she spotted the phone number Baines had given her.

She sent a text first. Not because he'd suggested it, but because she wasn't a monster.

This is Sp Agt Grace Reed of the AR St Pol Crim Investigations Div. I heard UR looking for UR roommate May I call you?

Three dots appeared. At work but take my break in 5. Can I call U

Grace tapped out a quick Okay and set her phone aside. Sure enough, five minutes later, it rang.

"CID, Special Agent Reed speaking," she said, trying to inject a modicum of warmth into her voice.

"Um, hi," a tentative female voice replied.

Grace picked up her pen and poised it over her notebook. She looked down at the notes she'd scrawled earlier and registered the missing girl's age. The caller came across as painfully young. She also sounded… genuinely worried.

"Yes? Hello, is this Kelli?"

"Yeah. Hi. I'm sorry to bother you," the caller began hesitantly. "She's probably flaking out on me—"

"It's no bother," Grace assured her, gently cutting her off. "Tell me what you know."

"Uh, well, my roommate hasn't come home in a few days, and when I called Stubby's, the place she works, they told me they haven't seen her since Friday night."

Grace frowned and jotted down the name of the missing person's employer, then circled *Friday* on the notes she'd taken from Baines as the day last seen. "And her name is Mallory?"

"Yes. Mallory Murray." The young woman hesitated for a moment. "To be honest, this isn't the first time she's taken off for a couple days, but usually she messages me something, you know?"

"And she hasn't been in touch?" Grace prompted, shifting to the edge of her seat.

"No. Nothing," the roommate said. "I tried texting her, because…" She trailed off. "Well, because she owes her half of the electric, and I have to pay the bill tomorrow," she finished in a rush. "She's tried to dodge bills in the past, but I'm not even getting read receipts."

"I understand," Grace said. And she did. "You've heard nothing from her since…?"

There was a pause on the other end. "I don't think I've actually spoken to her since Wednesday," she said. "We aren't really friends," she added easily. "I had a room to rent, and she answered the ad. She's only lived with me for three months."

And three months had been long enough for Kelli Simon to determine her roommate was less than reliable. "And you say it's not unusual for her to take off for a few days?"

"Yeah, but I mean, I can usually track her down at

work eventually. Besides, she wouldn't miss a Saturday shift at Stubby's. She says she gets her biggest tips on Saturdays."

"And Stubby's is…?"

She let the question hang out there, and Ms. Simon jumped on it. "Oh, it's a place out on Highway 62. Burgers, beers. Lots of lake people come in on weekends," she explained. "She's a waitress there. Occasionally bartender, depending on who's working."

"And she likes her job?"

There was a beat of silence. "I, uh, I have no idea," she admitted at last. "I guess. She brags about the cute guys who come in, and the tips and stuff."

"Do you know if she was seeing someone in particular?"

"No, not really. I mean, I'd hear her on the phone and stuff, and I know she went out a lot."

"Any names?"

"Maybe a Chad or something?" She paused. "And a Steve, but I think he was someone she worked with because she complained about him. I remember coming home early one day last week because my schedule opened up and she was on the phone with Steve asking if someone called Troy, or Trey, had come in."

"Troy or Trey," Grace murmured as she added the names to her notes. Curious, she asked, "And what do you do, Ms. Simon?"

"Me? I'm a nail tech. I work at a day spa here in town. The Lotus Flower?"

She spoke the name in an offhand sort of way indicating Grace should have heard of it. She hadn't. Each Criminal Investigation Division covered far more area than most people realized. Fort Smith was two hours away from the resort town of Eureka Springs. And even if she lived closer, Grace wasn't exactly the type to frequent spas, much to her sister's chagrin.

Grace read over her notes. "Has her family heard from her? Do you know?"

"As far as I know, she has a brother. She said her mom and dad died in a car wreck. I don't think she and her brother get along, though."

"No?"

"She says he's a jerk. Stuck-up. He's a hotshot attorney over in Bentonville."

"Do you know his name?"

Another silence followed. Finally, she said, "If she told me, I don't remember it. Maybe it started with an *M*, too? I remember thinking it was too much alliteration when she told me. Anyway, I don't think they were in touch often."

Grace got the distinct impression this well of information was tapped out, but still, she needed to follow up. Shouldn't be hard to find her brother if he actually was a lawyer.

Then again, maybe they'd all get lucky and Ms. Murray would find her way home on her own. "I see. Would tomorrow be a good day for us to talk in person?"

"In person?" the young woman questioned, like it hadn't occurred to her more than one conversation might be necessary.

"I'm based out of Fort Smith, but I could be in Eureka Springs by midmorning," Grace offered, not letting her off the hook.

"I have to work tomorrow," Kelli protested.

"Perhaps we can talk on your lunch hour." Grace wrote *Lotus Flower spa* on her pad and pushed on. "I'll text you in the morning and you can tell me when you'll be free. Please let me know if you hear from Ms. Murray."

After ending the call, she emailed her section chief to inform him she'd be out of the office the next day. Then she sent up a silent prayer for the missing young woman and closed her notebook. The photo of sweet Treveon Robinson beamed out at her from her monitor.

Leaning in, she stared intently at the screen. "Hang in there. I'll find you, little guy. I promise."

With a heavy sigh, she minimized the photo and opened her web browser. How many attorneys named Murray could there be in the Bentonville area? Seconds later, a networking website called WhosIn gave her the answer.

There were two. The first listing she found was for a personal injury attorney named Allen Murray, but when she clicked the link to his firm's website, she found a photo of a balding man in his sixties.

The other lawyer was named Matthew. Clicking on a link for more info, she mentally chalked one up to Ms. Kelli Simon and her linguistic pet peeves. It appeared Matthew Murray was an assistant prosecuting attorney for Benton County.

There was no photo, but Grace knew in her gut this had to be the brother. And now that she'd located him, she picked up her phone and prepared herself to be the bearer of bad news.

Chapter Two

Matthew Murray was not having a good day. First, the barista at the coffee shop he'd been visiting every day for the past two years screwed up his order. Again. While he didn't mind starting his day with a hearty double shot of espresso, or even an Americano heavy with cream and sugar, he absolutely did not want the sickeningly sweet barely coffee-flavored drink he'd ended up with. If asked under oath, he'd swear at least a third of the cup was filled with foam.

The morning didn't get any better. He had an appearance with Judge Walton in the earliest time slot, and if there was ever someone who was less of a morning person than Matthew, it was Judge Anthony Walton. The judge wasn't one of Matthew's biggest fans.

On his first day working for the Benton County prosecuting attorney's office, Matthew had backed out of a tight parking space and bumped the car behind him. Not enough of an impact to cause any damage, but enough to make him wince as he pulled away.

Unfortunately, the car behind his belonged to the judge. And Judge Walton happened to be standing on the sidewalk watching the whole thing. A summons to His Honor's chambers was dispatched within the hour.

But whether Judge Walton liked him or not was immaterial. The case he'd been handed three weeks ago was a mess. The sheriff's deputies who'd pulled Harley Jenkins over had not followed protocol when they searched his pickup truck. Therefore, the seizure of the cranky old hippie's pot stash, while impressive, was not quite legal. Still, Jenkins had enough of a rap sheet for the PA to insist on prosecuting the case.

Or rather, on Matthew prosecuting the case.

Harley Jenkins called himself an activist, but in actuality he was simply an agitator, a man whose own belief system seemed to change with the prevailing winds. The only thing Jenkins truly shared with the other men living their hardscrabble lives in the hills north of Beaver Lake was disdain for the law. Local, state, federal— it didn't matter. They believed themselves to be above any form of regulation.

For the most part, they wanted to be left alone. Matthew wished the overzealous young sheriff's deputy who'd pulled old Harley over had obliged. The judge threw out the evidence collected during the botched search, dismissed the case, then proceeded to give Matthew a good old-fashioned dressing-down he expected to be passed along to his boss, Prosecuting Attorney Nathaniel Able.

Matthew poked his head around Nate's office door and found the PA sitting with his head bent over his laptop, fingers flying as he stared at the screen, engrossed by whatever he was composing.

"I have a message for you from the jurist voted least

likely to enjoy having his time wasted," Matthew announced.

Nate jumped and jerked his hands from the keys. "Oh?" He sat back in his chair, dropping a mask of indifference over his initial surprise.

"Judge Walton dismissed the case against Harley Jenkins and said I was to tell you if we don't know any better than to push something like this onto his docket, he will personally lead the campaign opposing your reelection."

Nate's mouth twitched into a bemused half smile. "Excellent. If he raises a whole lot of money for my opponent, I won't have to do a bunch of rubber-chicken dinners to try to land this crap job again."

Matthew forced a slice of a smile and turned away. The two of them came from completely different worlds, and though he had political ambitions of his own, he wasn't sure he had it in him to go about it as determinedly as Nate.

His boss had once been northwest Arkansas's most highly recruited quarterback. He'd made the roster of a perennial favorite for the NCAA championship but never moved beyond the second string. In his junior year, he'd been savvy enough to start hunkering down and hitting the books. From there, he went straight from undergrad to law school, all funded by his proud parents and backed by hometown pride.

Matthew stopped by the coffee station to brew himself a cup of real coffee. His own upbringing had been about as jinxed as Nate's was charmed.

One of the ever-changing roster of law students who cycled through the office on internships hurried up to him as the machine gurgled to life. "Mr. Murray?" she asked, approaching him cautiously.

Matthew forced his smile into something more congenial. Tara? Tiffany? Trina? Her name started with a *T.* "Yeah? Hi, um…" He snapped his fingers twice, then gave up with a cringing smile. He hated being the guy who didn't learn people's names but believed it was worse to be the one who pretended he remembered. "I'm sorry, I forgot your name."

"Tia," she supplied.

"Yes! Tia!" He tapped his temple twice like he might hammer her name into a slot, but he knew she'd likely be gone from the office before it embedded. "Sorry. Hi, Tia."

He paused long enough to grab his now-full mug from under the spout. "And I'm Matthew. *Mr. Murray* makes me sound old." The second the words were out, he cringed on the inside. Now he sounded like a creeper. "I mean, I probably seem old to you, but I'm only twenty-nine."

"Oh, yeah. Um, right," she said quickly. "Twenty-nine is not old at all."

But her rushed delivery made her words sound insincere. To Tia, twenty-nine was ancient, he was sure. "Did you need me for something?" he asked, anxious to steer the conversation onto a more professional track.

"Oh! Yeah. You had a message from an investigator with the state police," she said, thrusting a sticky note at him. "She said she left you a voice mail but wanted to be sure you got back to her today, if possible."

Matthew frowned at the slip of paper. *Special Agent Grace Reed—ASP* was written in looping handwriting.

Beneath it a phone number printed in deliberately neat blocks. He thought of his own message-taking skills and wondered if Tia had recopied the name and number from a more hastily scrawled version. Either way, he appreciated the effort.

"Thank you, Tia." He saluted her with his mug. "I'll give Special Agent, uh, Reed a call as soon as I can."

"You're welcome," the young intern called after him.

Once he reached his office, he set the mug on a stoneware razorback coaster and stuck the note to the center of his computer monitor. He docked his laptop, booted everything up and surveyed at the array of printed affidavits and files piled atop his desk. *Paperless office*, he thought and scoffed. The law would never be paperless.

To his left, the green light indicating he had a voice mail on his desk phone was flashing. He hit the speaker button and ran through the prompts to access his messages.

"Hello, Mr. Murray, this is Grace Reed with the Arkansas State Police Criminal Investigation Division out of Fort Smith. I'm wondering if you can tell me if you might be related to a young woman named Mallory Murray? If you are, would you please give me a call as soon as you receive this message? I would appreciate it. My number is…"

Mallory.

The state police were calling him about Mallory. They wanted to know if he knew Mallory. His troublesome baby sister was the subject of a phone call from the Criminal Investigation Division. Matthew sagged, allowing his shoulders to slump with the weight of his failure as he leaned forward and propped his forehead in the palm of his hand.

What had she done now? How much trouble was she in? And how much of it would blow back on him?

He knew the last question didn't exactly make him a candidate for brother of the year, but his relationship with his sister had long been rocky at best and downright combative in the low spots. When they'd last spoken, Mallory had told him to butt out of her life, and he'd been more than happy to do as she asked.

From the day she was born, they were oil and water. He'd been five—almost six—and couldn't understand why his parents were bringing this new baby into their perfect world. He knew his mother hadn't wanted another baby. He'd heard his parents talking about it, but like everyone else figured she'd come around to the idea. But from the moment they brought Mallory home, there was a new tension in the household.

Their upbringing had been what he'd call barely middle-class. His dad had a decent management job with a company that made truck parts, and his mom was an elementary school librarian. There'd never been a lot of money, but they'd scrimped and saved enough to send him to the University of Arkansas, with the help of a couple scholarships and a student loan. He figured the age gap between him and Mallory kept them from ever feeling truly close. Sadly, the gap grew into a gorge after their parents were killed in a car crash.

It happened two weeks prior to his undergrad graduation. Mallory had only been in eleventh grade. He'd already been accepted to law school but had deferred a year to help get his sister through her senior year. Not that she'd ever thanked him for putting his life on hold for her. Quite the opposite, in fact.

Mallory resented his role as guardian. She believed she was grown enough to be out on her own. On the day of her high school graduation, he'd handed over the keys to the house they'd grown up in, assuring her he had enough to cover the mortgage for at least a year. Feeling his job was done, he headed for Little Rock and law school with only the things he could fit in his car. She'd managed to hang onto the house for about a year before they were forced to sell.

Their attempts at togetherness usually took place around the holidays, when one or both of them was feeling lonely or nostalgic for the kind of Christmases they'd never had but saw on TV. More often than not, they ended with Mallory either begging him for money or blaming him for her bad choices. Or both. Inevitably, they also ended with one of them taking off, harsh words still hanging between them.

She'd always been reckless when it came to choosing the company she kept. He'd been able to help her out of a couple minor scrapes with the law, but they'd been nothing warranting more than a fine and an appearance in front of a judge.

But the state police criminal investigations people... they handled major crime. The kind of crime most rural sheriffs' departments were ill-equipped to tackle. If they were calling, Mallory had pushed her luck too far.

Picking up his phone, he carefully punched out the digits on the sticky note. It rang twice before a no-nonsense female voice answered. "CID, Grace Reed speaking."

Matthew got the sense he was interrupting her. He could almost feel her annoyance emanating across the line. "Special Agent Reed, this is Matthew Murray. You left a message for me to call?"

"Oh." He heard a quiet exhalation. "Yes, sorry," she said, softening her tone. "Matthew Murray," she repeated, obviously switching gears. "Are you related to a young woman named Mallory Murray, by chance?"

"Yes, Mallory is my sister," he replied, keeping his pitch as even as possible. "Is there something I can help you with?"

"Well, uh, I hate giving this sort of news over the phone, but—"

Matthew tensed. When his parents had been killed, a police officer had been dispatched to the off-campus apartment he shared with two other guys. He was glad whatever bad news Special Agent Reed had to deliver could be transmitted via telephone.

"Go ahead," he prompted, snapping his mouth shut when he caught the creak in his voice.

"This morning I received a call from a young woman named Kelli Simon. She says she shares an apartment with your sister in Eureka Springs," she began. "She called the Carroll County Sheriff's Department this morning because your sister has not been seen since Friday."

Matthew was glad Special Agent Reed couldn't see him slump in relief at the news his sister was simply missing and not dead. He knew as well as anyone missing persons were often at risk, but it wasn't at all unusual for Mallory to disappear when it suited her. Exhaling long and slow, he forced himself to focus.

"Did she take anything with her? Did the roommate notice if she packed clothes or anything?"

"No," Agent Reed replied. "As far as Ms. Simon could tell, your sister left the apartment on Friday intending to go to work at a place called Stubby's on Highway 62, but she never came home. Her calls are going to voice mail, and she hasn't replied to any text messages."

Matthew sat back in his chair and pinched the bridge of his nose. At last, he raked his fingers through his hair. "Has she posted anything? Mallory loves to post pictures on social media." *Mainly pictures of herself*, he added silently. "PicturSpam is her favorite, I think, but there's always a new one."

Sitting up straight, he clicked on his web browser and typed in the address for the social media platform. He wasn't active on it himself, but he had an account, and he and his sister had followed one another there before the latest fallout. Unless she'd blocked him, he should be able to see if she had made any recent posts.

"I've been able to access her public profile, but she may have some friends-only content I can't see," Special Agent Reed reported.

Matthew bit back the urge to tell her it was unlikely. Anything Mallory did, she wanted the whole world to see.

"The last post I could see was of the night sky, and it looked like the moon reflecting off the lake," the investigator continued. "It was posted Friday evening and geotagged near Table Rock Lake. Do you know if your sister has any friends in the area?"

Matthew found himself staring at the same image Grace Reed had described, but he was embarrassingly clueless as to whom Mallory kept company with. "No. I mean, I don't know," he said quickly. "We haven't been particularly close in recent years."

There was a pause on the other end of the line, and for a moment Matthew wondered if Grace Reed with all her superior detective skills had already deduced as much.

"Mr. Murray, unless your sister resurfaces in the next twelve hours, I'm planning to head to Eureka Springs tomorrow morning to meet with Ms. Simon and see their apartment. Perhaps there might be a clue left behind. Would you like to accompany me?"

Matthew swallowed hard. Would he like to? No. Should he? Probably. He hesitated, loath to admit to this stranger he was probably the last person who would be able to give any real insight into his sister's life, but it was true. They might have been siblings, but they weren't friends. Certainly not confidants.

Their lives had taken completely divergent paths, and Matthew could admit, if only to himself, he hadn't minded Mallory's absence. His sister was drama. His sister incited chaos.

His sister was missing.

Part of him wanted to bristle at the thought of chasing after her. There was nothing Mallory loved more than tension, and this was the sort of thing to rev her up. But what if… What if something had gone wrong? What if someone had abducted her, or worse?

Matthew shook his head, refusing to let himself go too far down the dark path yet. It was better for him to believe Mallory was off on one of her lost weekends. She had likely flaked out on the roommate and her job.

His baby sister was an attention-seeking young woman with aspirations beyond her current circumstances. She'd always leap at a chance to graze greener pastures.

"Yes," he said after the pause had lasted a few seconds too long. "Uh, I would like to go with you, but I'm not sure I can get someone to cover my workload tomorrow morning." He hedged, tapping his pen against the pile of case notes and files.

He had another case in front of Judge Walton at nine, and the winding drive over the hills from Bentonville to the resort town of Eureka Springs would take an hour or more. Plus, he wasn't sure he was the right person to be meeting Mallory's roommate or pawing through her things. Heaven only knew what kind of fabrications she'd woven about their relationship.

"It's fine." Agent Reed dropped her voice into a confidential pitch. "Truthfully, I'm not sure the roommate wants to meet with me, and if we both show up, it might make her even less forthcoming." He heard the click of a computer mouse. "How about I come to Bentonville after I'm done speaking to Ms. Simon? I'd like to stop by this Stubby's place on my way. Perhaps by then I'll have more to tell you."

"Sounds good," Matthew replied, relieved to be exempted from the information gathering. "Are you thinking mid- to late afternoon?" he hazarded.

"Yes, most likely," she answered.

"Great. Come to the prosecuting attorney's offices when you get to town. I'll be here until at least seven or later."

"Perfect. See you tomorrow."

She ended the call without another word, and Matthew fell back in his seat. He stared at the ceiling, the phone still clutched in his hand. Mallory was missing. And he must be missing something, too, because the only emotion he could identify was irritation.

He truly must be an awful brother, he thought, shaking his head at himself.

Chapter Three

The Lotus Flower spa looked like the type of place Grace promised her sister they'd visit but never booked. She scanned the salon as she stood in the dimly lit reception area. She couldn't imagine checking in and telling the perky young woman wearing a headset she was there for some kind of Andean mud treatment or whatever new age services they offered. While she wasn't opposed to a massage after a hard workout, she couldn't picture herself booking an appointment at a place like this. It was too…perfect.

When she arrived, she'd simply flashed her credentials and asked to speak to Kelli Simon. The receptionist had been mildly freaked out the minute she'd introduced herself. She tried to reassure the young woman Kelli was not in any sort of trouble, but the panic on her face told Grace it didn't matter. Within minutes the entire staff would know someone from the state police had come to question one of their nail technicians.

"Agent Reed?" a petite red-haired woman said as she stepped through a door concealed in the wall.

Grace stifled the urge to jump and forced her mouth into a smile. "I didn't even see that door."

"I'm Kelli Simon," the young woman said, offering her hand. "Would you mind if we spoke outside?"

Grace gestured to the door. "Not at all. Lead the way."

Ms. Simon walked quickly past her and outside. Grace trailed. Kelli then hooked a right and headed for a coffee shop two doors down. Nodding to the entrance, she spared Grace a sheepish glance. "Do you mind if I run in and get a cappuccino? I'd be happy to order something for you."

"No, thank you." Grace gestured to one of the umbrella-shaded tables. "Why don't you grab your drink and I'll wait for you out here."

"Perfect," Kelli replied, ducking into the shop. "Be right back."

Grace wouldn't have minded a cold bottle of water, but she wanted to keep the meeting on more of a business footing than a social call. Grace was all too aware this meeting could be the start of an intense investigation. It was important to put Ms. Simon at ease, but she had to keep moving forward quickly.

She settled onto the hard metal chair and pulled a notebook and pen from her tote bag. She carried an electronic tablet with her, but found good old-fashioned note-taking seemed to make people more comfortable. People tended to stiffen up when they saw you typing information into a document in a way they didn't when they saw you make a quick note with a pen. She would transcribe the pertinent information into the electronic case file she'd share with her division and the county sheriff's office later.

Kelli Simon returned a few minutes later with an enormous paper cup in hand. She settled into the seat across from Grace and clasped the coffee between her fingers like she needed it to warm them despite temperatures already inching into the nineties.

Grace made note of the young woman's defensive posture and smiled as warmly as she could. "Thank you for seeing me today."

"You're welcome. I took my lunch early," she explained, glancing over her shoulder at the spa.

"There's nothing to be nervous about," Grace assured her, slanting a glance at the other woman's grip on the cup. "I'm only going to ask a few questions."

"Sorry." The apology seemed to be her usual opening gambit to any conversation, but she released her stranglehold on the cup. "They keep it freezing in the spa, and my hands are always wet. It can be hard to get them warm."

"Ah, I see." Grace nodded and offered another encouraging smile. "I totally understand. I'm often one of the only women in whatever office I'm working in, and the men tend to set the thermostat to meat-locker level. I keep a heater under my desk, and I've been known to run it all summer long."

Her confession seemed to help the younger woman relax. Lifting the cup, she took a quick sip, then placed it back on the filigreed metal table with exaggerated care.

"I still haven't heard anything from her," she said quietly.

"I'm sorry to hear that," Grace responded. She clicked open her pen and made a note on the pad. *Mallory Murray still missing as of Tuesday 11:24 a.m.* "No contact from anyone looking for her or asking about her?"

The other woman shook her head. "We didn't have

friends in common. I'm not sure anyone she knows would have my number." She shrugged. "I did go through some of her things," she offered hesitantly. "In her room."

Intrigued, Grace leaned in. "Oh?"

She let the single syllable hang out there between them, knowing the other woman would feel compelled to fill the silence.

"Yeah. I didn't find a whole lot, but I can tell you her brother's name is definitely Matthew. I found some paperwork that had both of their names on it."

Grace nodded but didn't offer up the fact she had already tracked down Matthew Murray. "What kind of paperwork?"

Kelli shrugged. "Legal-looking stuff? I think it had something to do with the sale of a house. Maybe their parents' house?" She opened her hands in a gesture to show she was guessing. "I don't know. I'm no expert."

"How long have you and Mallory been roommates?"

"About three months?" Again, she phrased her statement like a question. Grace wouldn't be able to refute any fact she put out there; she simply nodded and made note of it.

"And you guys met through…"

"A roommate service," Kelli answered, looking slightly abashed. "You know, online?"

Her pitch climbed again, and Grace wondered if the girl ever spoke in anything but interrogatories. "What kind of information did you exchange prior to deciding to sublet to her?"

"You know, the usual. Where she had a job, where she lived, if she had any problems with other roommates, if she smoked." She threw the last one out there as if this line of inquiry should be obvious to anyone.

"None of her answers raised any red flags? You said she'd been dodgy on paying some of the bills?"

Kelli nodded but shifted it into another shake of her head. "Not at first, but yeah. It was always something like she was in between paychecks or her tips weren't as good on a Saturday as she thought they would be. Usually, she would only need me to float her for a day or two," she explained. "But she always paid…eventually," she was quick to add.

Grace got the distinct impression Kelli Simon thought if she said anything too negative about her relationship with Mallory Murray, or showed any discord between them, it might make her a suspect. Hoping to build rapport, she set her pen down and nodded as she leaned in.

"I had a roommate like her in college," Grace informed her. "It's never their fault, but they can never get it together. That type of thing?" She let her voice rise on the last part, imitating Kelli's speech pattern in the hopes of ingratiating herself to the young woman.

"Exactly," Kelli responded immediately, sitting up straighter.

Grace smiled, pleased her ploy had worked. "I think we've all been there." She scribbled the words *late paying bills* on her notepad. "You said she might be seeing someone. When you looked through her stuff, did you find anything more about this guy she was seeing?"

Kelli bit her bottom lip, clearly wrestling with a decision. Sensing the other woman's desire to spill, Grace pressed gently.

"Anything at all."

"I cleaned the apartment the other night," the younger woman began. "I usually do on Sundays. I like to start the week fresh, you know?"

Grace thought of her own somewhat haphazard housekeeping. "Yeah, totally." When Kelli hesitated again, she pushed harder but focused her gaze on her notepad. She didn't want to scare the girl off. "Did you find something? Maybe something related to this mystery guy?"

"Well…" She drew on her poor abused lip again, then blurted, "I found a pregnancy test."

Grace's head popped up. "A pregnancy test? A used one?" This case might've been a whole lot more involved than what she had initially believed.

Kelli nodded but did not speak.

"And did it have a result?"

"Positive," the other woman whispered.

"Was it only the one test?" Grace asked, her gaze locked on the younger woman. "I believe some people take multiples to be sure."

"The box in the trash said there were two tests, but I only saw one of the stick things in it," Kelli asserted.

Grace let the information sink in. If the second test had come back positive as well, it was entirely possible Mallory had held on to it to show the father of her baby. And if the father of her baby was not the kind of man to be excited about such news, things may not have gone the way Mallory had planned.

"But you didn't find anything in her room? Nothing identifying the guy she was seeing by name? No cards or notes or anything?"

Kelli shook her head. "Nothing."

Grace made a note in her book. *Pregnant?* She underlined the word twice, drew arrows stemming from it. At the end of one she wrote the word *yes*, and at the end of the other she wrote the word *no*.

"Did she talk to you about this guy? Has she posted anything about him on social media? Given any indication as to whether he might be serious about her?" she hedged.

"No." Kelli wagged her head hard. "Like I said, we weren't friends at all. I sent her a request on PicturSpam not long after she moved in, but she never confirmed the follow. I got embarrassed and deleted the request."

Grace nodded. Social media was a minefield on multiple levels, but often in her line of work it turned out to be a gold mine.

"Okay. Well, I was able to locate her brother yesterday and reached out to him. He hasn't heard from her, either, but like you said, he told me they weren't close. I'm heading over to Bentonville when I leave here to talk to him, but I'm wondering if you would mind if I took a quick peek at your apartment."

Kelli looked taken aback by the suggestion. "My apartment?"

Grace raised one eyebrow. "Yes." She closed her notebook. "I realize you're on your lunch hour, but I would appreciate it if I could at least see her room. Maybe you could show me the papers and box you found? I assume you kept them."

Kelli nodded. "Yes, I did. I didn't know… I wasn't sure if I should tell you. Heck, for all I know, it might not have even been Mallory's. She could have had a friend over or something."

Grace forced herself to smile and nod. Not a reasonable scenario, but she didn't want to slow her down. "Right, we don't know for certain."

Kelli inclined her head. "Okay, but I'll have to make it quick." She checked her phone. "I have an appointment booked in at one, and I need to get back to set up."

The metal feet of her chair scraped the sidewalk as Grace rose. "Do you live far from here? I can drive if you'd like," she offered.

Her search on the address Kelli had given showed they lived close to the spa. Still, she didn't want Kelli to feel like she was the one under investigation.

Kelli shook her head. "No need. It's only a few blocks. We could probably walk there faster."

Grace allowed Kelli to lead the way. "Must be nice to live this close to your work," she said as they turned onto a side street. Hoping to find a common thread with the now-skittish young woman, she offered some information of her own. "I have about a ten-minute drive every day, but some mornings it feels like thirty."

"We don't open until after ten, so most people are already at work," Kelli said. "But yeah, I like being able to walk to work. I used to go home for lunch just to get out for a while," she said with a shrug. She cast a shy glance at Grace. "Lately, I've been taking my lunch to work more often. It's kind of awkward to come home while she's there."

"Mallory didn't work during the day?"

"Her schedule changed a lot," Kelli replied. "Mostly evenings, but on weekends she'd pull a double because she liked the tips."

Grace matched her stride to Kelli's hurried pace. "And when you said it was awkward…?"

Again, the girl let one shoulder rise and fall. "She was there," she said, feigning nonchalance. "I, uh, I like to eat my lunch alone. I have to make conversation with clients all day long, and lunch is about the only hour I get to, you know, just be."

"I see."

Grace hummed. She did understand the younger woman's need to have space to breathe during the workday. She often felt the same herself. It wasn't easy being the only woman on her shift. There were days the conversations in the break room made her uncomfortable. Not because the guys said anything overt. They were all too well trained to go too far, but because she knew she didn't quite fit in. Even if she could talk baseball, football or basketball with most any man, she was always the token female in the conversation.

"Well, I appreciate you meeting with me today. And for caring enough to make the call to the police to start. It's not easy trying to piece together what you know about a person you barely know. I spend my days doing it, and it can be frustrating."

Kelli pointed to a brick duplex on the right. "This is me. Us, I mean," she corrected quickly. "And, yeah, it's kind of weird. I guess I thought maybe we'd become friends?"

Again she finished on a high note. Grace got the feeling she was asking if her expectations had been unrealistic.

"I get you."

"Anyway, early on, Mallory made it pretty clear she

had her own thing going on and didn't want to get too friendly."

"What do you mean by her own thing?" Grace asked as the other woman unlocked the door to the duplex.

Kelli led the way into an apartment Grace would have said was decorated in early-twenty-something chic. The furniture was mainly comprised of castoffs or hand-me-downs, but dressed up with colorful paint or, in the case of the sofa, an artfully tucked slipcover.

"She preferred to hang out with the people she knew from work, I guess," Kelli said, sounding dejected. "Most of the people I work with are married or engaged. I'm not seeing anyone right now, and I thought she wasn't, so I figured we could hang out or go out together, but Mallory wasn't interested."

Grace bobbed her head in understanding. "Too bad. You seem pretty nice. I'm going to go out on a limb and say it was probably her loss."

Kelli clutched her coffee cup to her chest. "Yeah, her loss." She nodded to the narrow hallway off the living room. "Mallory's room is the one at the end of the hall, right across from the bathroom. There's not much in there, but I guess it won't hurt for you to take a look around."

"I did get her brother's permission, if that makes you feel better."

She stepped back and gestured for Grace to proceed. "I put the box with the test in the medicine cabinet. I figured if she showed up, I'd toss it in the trash and she'd never know I saw it."

Grace headed down the hall. "Thank you, but I'll

want to take it with me in case we can get any forensic information from it."

Behind her, Kelli gasped. "I didn't think about fin- gerprints. I didn't touch it, I swear. I mean, I touched the box, but not the test thingy. I used a tissue," she amended as she hurried after Grace. "I mean, she, uh, urinated on it, and I didn't want to touch anything, you know, kinda gross," she babbled.

"It's okay," Grace assured her as she stepped into the bathroom.

She opened the medicine cabinet and eyeballed the box. Sure enough, it claimed to include two tests. Rather than reaching for it, she turned to Kelli, who hovered in the doorway clutching her coffee cup.

"Do you have a plastic bag handy? Something with a zip top? Like a freezer bag?" She had a couple of ev- idence bags in her purse, but asking Kelli to find one would send the young woman to the kitchen and give her a moment alone in the space.

"Be right back," Kelli promised.

Grace leaned in and caught the open end of the box with her pen. Turning it in her direction, she could see Kelli hadn't been wrong. There was only one plastic stick in the box. She tipped the box over and peered down at the window on the wand. Plus sign.

A montage of different scenarios played in her head.

Mallory was unhappy about the pregnancy and had gone off to determine if she should go through with it?

The boyfriend was happy about the possibility of a baby and they'd hopped a plane to Vegas?

The boyfriend was unhappy and Mallory was now consigned to parts unknown?

The younger woman returned holding a gallon bag with a slider top, and Grace jerked herself out of her reverie.

"Perfect. Thank you," Grace said as she used the pen to lift the box from the cabinet and secure it in the bag. Then she dropped the whole thing into her tote and craned her neck to peer over Kelli's shoulder toward the room across the hall.

"Her room?"

"Oh." The young woman moved to let Grace pass. "Yes, this is hers. I kept the master because I pay more in rent, and—"

Not needing to hear more, Grace held up a hand as she passed. "I won't be long, I promise."

Kelli hadn't exaggerated. Mallory's room contained a mattress and box spring on the floor. The dresser and nightstand appeared to come from one of those kits you have to put together with a wrench that doesn't fit anything else in the world. The rest of the space was filled with clothes.

Tons of clothes.

Stepping over the mounds on the floor and ignoring the cascade of apparel spilling out of the closet, Grace immediately went to the nightstand and opened the drawer. There she found the usual detritus—hair elastics, bills, receipts, a couple of condoms in wrappers, a paperback romance novel and assorted lip balms. But beneath it all there appeared to be a folder embossed with the logo of a title company.

She pulled it from under the rest. "Was this the paperwork you found?" she asked, glancing over her shoulder at Kelli.

The younger woman blushed, obviously embarrassed to have been caught trying to cover up her snooping. "Yes."

Grace opened the folder and scanned the documents. They did indeed reference Mallory and Matthew Murray as the owners of a piece of property near Garfield, Arkansas.

"You're right. Looks like they sold some property they owned jointly."

Kelli nodded. "She told me she'd grown up over near Beaver Lake. I didn't put it together until I saw that folder."

"Put what together?" Grace asked, curious.

"You know, living here in Eureka but working at a place like Stubby's. She's into the whole lake life thing. Likes hanging out with the people who come up for the weekends."

"Like guys named Chad or Troy?"

Kelli wrinkled her nose. "Well, yeah. I mean, they sound like rich-person names, don't they?" Kelli gave a snort of derision. "All the guys I knew growing up were named Junior or Bubba or something like that."

Kelli had a point. Her mind flashed to Treveon, and she couldn't help marveling at how much weight something as seemingly innocuous as a name could have.

"You're right. Good thinking. I'll ask her brother if he has any ideas."

She did another circuit of the room, peering into the cluttered closet, then returning to the nightstand drawer and checking through it again. Convinced she had the most pertinent of clues stashed in a plastic bag, she smiled at Kelli Simon as she nodded her satisfaction with her search. "I'll get out of your hair and let you get back to work."

The younger woman exhaled, the tension in her stance visibly dissipating for a moment. She glanced at the fitness tracker strapped to her wrist and snapped to attention again. "Oh. Yeah, I'm sorry. I really do have to get back," she said, eyes widening.

Grace gave the apartment's common areas another once-over as they passed through. None of the chaos from Mallory's room spilled over. Either Kelli Simon had done an excellent job of her Sunday cleaning or her roommate rarely availed herself to the rest of the space.

As they exited the duplex and Kelli turned to lock the door, Grace gave the other woman a more deliberate inspection. Kelli was pretty in a girl-next-door sort of way. She possessed none of the languid beauty Mallory Murray projected in the photos emailed to her. The two seemed an odd pairing. Then again, Kelli herself had admitted they weren't actually friends.

"Thank you again," Grace said, extending a hand. "Please call me if you hear anything from Mallory. If I discover anything of note, I'll be sure to be in touch."

"I'd appreciate that," Kelli replied. She shifted her weight from one foot to the other. "I, uh—" she gestured down the hill toward the business district "— have to go."

"Go on ahead." Grace pointed in the opposite direction. "I couldn't find street parking, so I'm in a spot up here." Waving the younger woman on, she turned and headed for the other end of the block. Around the corner, she waited until she was certain Kelli was gone, then doubled back.

Moving at a more methodical pace, Grace took in everything she could about the street where Mallory Murray lived. She checked each gray car she passed to be sure it wasn't the five-year-old subcompact her brother said she drove. Not one of them had a window sticker that read, Sweet 'n' Sassy Southern Girl. Satisfied she'd ascertained all she could there, she climbed into her own car, programmed her navigation for Stubby's Bar and Grill, and headed west out of Eureka Springs.

Chapter Four

Matthew wasn't quite sure what he'd imagined Special Agent Grace Reed to look like when he'd spoken to her on the phone, but whatever image his brain had conjured, it came nowhere near the reality of her.

She was tall. Approaching six feet, he figured, by the way she nearly looked him straight in the eye as they shook hands. Her grip was firm and businesslike, but her dark brown hair fell loose past her shoulders in soft waves. Her gray slacks, silky T-shirt and neatly tailored blazer showed off a figure he'd call lean rather than thin.

For a moment, he lost himself in the notion of her taking him down. He'd bet money she could do it. To his own surprise, he found the thought of it intriguing rather than emasculating.

"Would you like to have a seat?" he asked, gesturing to one of the chairs positioned in front of his desk.

"Yes, thank you," she said, stepping past him to claim a chair.

Out of nervousness and habit, Matthew buttoned his suit jacket as he circled his desk to return to his chair, only to quickly unbutton it again to sit. "I've not had any news from Mallory," he said without preamble. "Has her roommate heard anything more from her?"

Agent Reed shook her head. "No, she's not heard from her, either. I spoke to Ms. Simon and visited your sister's apartment. She hasn't been home."

The news stung more than Matthew thought it would. He sucked air in through his teeth but clamped his mouth shut. Years of law school had taught him listening usually garnered more answers than a barrage of questions. Agent Reed would get to what he needed to know.

"I stopped by Stubby's Bar and Grill on my way here, but Steve, the owner and person who was working the night Mallory disappeared, is out of town and won't be back until tomorrow. I'll go out there again and see if he can give any additional information."

Matthew nodded. He laced his fingers atop the blotter on his desk and found himself unable to meet Agent Reed's steady gaze. "I wish I had more information for you." He felt the color rise in his cheeks but didn't fight it.

He was Mallory's brother. He should be embarrassed he hadn't kept closer contact with his only sibling. "There's an age gap between me and Mallory. We've never been tight, but after our parents passed…" He let the rest of the thought drift away.

The detective nodded her understanding. "It happens."

"I've been racking my brain, trying to think back over the few conversations we have had in the past year or two." He sank back in his chair and pressed his fingertips to his forehead, smoothing his brows before letting his hands fall away. He looked up into her eyes and gave a helpless shrug.

"The fact of the matter is, we don't like each other much." One corner of his mouth lifted in a sardonic smile. "A horrible thing to say out loud, but it's true. She thinks I'm bossy and have a gigantic stick up my rear, and I think she's a… I don't know." He shifted his gaze, unable to maintain contact any longer. "A slacker, I guess."

She nodded, and he got the feeling she already knew all of this. It annoyed him. The notion that this stranger might have a better handle on his relationship with his only relative irked him enough to make him snap his mouth shut again.

But Agent Reed had other ideas.

"Tell me about her," she prompted, extracting her phone from her bag. "I'd like to record this, if you don't mind. I'll take notes, too, but once in a while people say things out loud they don't realize is important or gives us a clue," she explained.

Matthew stared at the phone for a moment, his gaze fixed on the red dot on the screen that would start recording their conversation. He knew anything he had to say could go on record if Agent Reed decided to turn her investigation in his direction, but he had nothing to hide.

"I agree. Please, start the recording."

Agent Reed set the phone on the desk and touched the button. She spoke her name, then noted the date and time of their conversation.

Before she could ask her first question, he jumped in. "I'd like to ask you whether you think I had anything to do with my sister's disappearance."

She looked up at him, her expression curious but unfazed. "*Should* I think you have something to do with your sister's disappearance?"

"No."

"I don't have any reason to believe you have been more connected to your sister than you claim," she concluded. "But I'm listening if you have a cause for concern."

Matthew gave his head a vigorous shake. "No. Nothing more than familial concern." He gave her a wry smile. "Call it lawyers' paranoia. We always get a bit nervous when there's going to be a record."

She returned his smile, and it made Matthew sit up in his chair again. In its resting state, her face was sober. Stoic. An attractive sculpture of a serious woman. But her smile transformed her entirely. The warmth of it made him want to answer any questions she fired at him. He wondered if Special Agent Grace Reed was aware her smile was her superpower.

Catching himself, he waved a hand to the phone and nodded. "Ask away, Agent Reed."

Her smile burned brighter for a moment, then she dimmed it down as she studied him closely. "We play on the same side of the law, Mr. Murray. How about for the sake of this conversation you call me Grace and I'll call you Matthew?"

Matthew sat forward, his shoulders relaxing at the invitation to informality. "Okay, Grace."

"Is there anything you want to tell me about your sister, Mallory? Anything at all."

Matthew closed his eyes, and the image that had been haunting him since he'd first spoken to Grace flashed into his mind. It was a photograph his parents had kept on the mantel in the house where they grew up. In it, Mallory was probably about seven or eight. She'd performed in her first dance recital. She wore one of those fluffy ballerina dresses with sparkles and sequins sewn into the fabric, a rhinestone tiara, and a smile a mile wide.

It was the image that sprang to mind whenever he thought of his sister. In the photo, Mallory was the star she'd always wanted to be.

"Mal is a pretty girl. Always has been. Like the kind of pretty people would stop my parents to comment on. When she was younger, she liked to dance, sing…perform, basically anything onstage," he said, his brow furrowing as he tried to shape memories into words. "She likes attention. There were six years between us, but when we were younger, she stuck to me like glue. I didn't pay as much attention to her as she would have liked."

When he paused, Grace smiled. "Naturally. I'm sure the clinginess annoyed you."

"Yeah, it did," he admitted with a rueful huff of a laugh. "She loved—loves," he corrected, "anything sparkly or glittery, which holds zero interest for me…"

"Please continue."

"My parents doted on her. After me, they didn't think they'd have any more kids. She was a surprise."

"Tell me about your parents. They were killed in a car crash?" she said, her gaze boring into his.

"Yes. They were your average parents," he said with a shrug. "Our dad worked as a manager at a machine shop, and Mom worked at the school. They never had a lot of money. They helped as much as they could when I went off to college, but I got some scholarships and financial aid. They contributed what they could," he said slowly, "but it wasn't much in the grand scheme of things. It wasn't until last year I realized that Mallory had the impression Mom and Dad were footing the bill for me to go to college."

"Oh?"

"She blames me. I was the reason she couldn't have a car on her sixteenth birthday or the clothes she wished she had." He paused, tucked chin to his chest as he pushed down the bewilderment and frustration he'd felt when his sister had finally unleashed years of resentment on him.

"I didn't realize because I was pretty far removed from the home situation, but my parents were struggling financially. Not because I was in school, though. My dad drank too much. My mother tended to get her revenge on him through the home shopping channels." He chuckled, but there was no humor to it. "It was a pattern our whole lives. I think maybe Mallory saw too much of their dysfunctional dynamic and didn't have an example of how to work hard to get what you want."

Agent Reed leaned forward in her chair, bracing her elbows on her knees. Her expression stayed neutral. "What makes you say so?"

"Mallory has…let's call it an overinflated sense of entitlement." The corner of his mouth ticked up, and he lifted his hands in a futile gesture he hoped indicated his cluelessness. "I'm not sure where she got it. We never had money. We never wore the cool shoes or played the latest video games. Our parents were able to cover the essentials, but not a whole lot of the extras. For some reason, Mallory got it into her head she was owed those extras, and it was my fault she never had them."

"Why do you think she blames you?"

He looked directly at her. "Because she told me she does."

"Bluntly? I mean, she said as much out loud?"

"Yes, ma'am." He saw her cringe at the *ma'am*. "Sorry, reflex."

She waved him off. "No problem. When was it she told you she thought you were the reason she couldn't have nice things?"

"When our parents were killed in the crash, there was a bit of life insurance, but not quite enough to cover the costs of burying both of them. We put the house up for sale. When it finally did sell, I used what we earned from the proceeds to pay off what we owed the funeral home and split any remaining profit. Mallory was furious."

Her brow puckered. "Why?"

"Because I didn't use my own money to pay the bill," he explained. "She figured since Mom and Dad had contributed to my college education but not hers—she wasn't out of high school when they died—she was owed a larger portion of the estate."

"I see."

"She didn't care about the mountain of debt I had from undergrad and the loans piling up from law school. It didn't matter how I explained things to her. She still ended up with a fairly decent lump sum after the dust settled, but nothing was ever enough for Mallory."

"And you feel this colored your relationship with your sister?"

"I know it did," he said succinctly. "We didn't get together often, but when we did, Mallory never failed to let me know she felt she was entitled to more."

"Did she ask you for money?"

He huffed a laugh. "Almost the minute I landed my first job. She wasn't interested in hearing about student loan payments."

"I assume whatever nest egg she had was gone?"

He nodded. "As far as I can tell, the only smart thing she did with the money was to buy a car. As for the rest, who knows where it went? She's come to me more than once asking to borrow money for security deposits on apartments. She rarely stays in one place for long."

"Do you give her money?"

He nodded. "I have in the past." He looked down at his clasped hands again and heaved a sigh. "I didn't when she called a few months ago. I told her she was old enough and should have her life more pulled together. I told her I was done with the handouts, and she told me she was done accepting scraps." He shook his head. "I can't help thinking about the picture."

"Picture?"

"My parents had a picture of her dressed up for a dance recital they kept on the mantel. You know, like the sparkly dress with the crown and everything?"

Grace nodded.

"I can't help wondering if maybe somehow my sister decided she was some kind of fairy-tale princess stuck in this life. Like Cinderella or Snow White. Like she was waiting for her prince to come along and rescue her.

I mean, it's not unusual for kids who grow up around here to be envious of the kids who come up here to the lake houses. Some of them are massive."

Grace shifted in her seat, easing back against the chair again. She uncrossed and recrossed her legs, and because he still had blood coursing through his veins, Matthew couldn't help but marvel at how long those legs were.

"Can you expound?" she asked, jolting him from his thoughts. "I'm not from around here, but I'm sure the lakes are a big draw. What's the relationship between the locals and the people who own places up here on the lakes?"

Unlacing his fingers, he opened his hands again and let his shoulders rise and fall. "It's a classic case of the haves versus the have-nots," he said without rancor. "When the Army Corps of Engineers built the dams on the White River, they created a playground for the wealthy by flooding the homesteads of the poor." He raised his eyebrows. "You've lived in Arkansas how long, Agent Reed?"

"My whole life," she answered immediately.

"Then I don't have to tell you this is a state of extremes, do I? There's money up here in northwest Arkansas, and lots more in Little Rock, but not much between. You might find a pocket of it here and there, but most of the people around here fall into the have-not category."

"True."

"Up here it tends to be more evident than in some places. People from all over come to the Ozarks, to these lakes. They like the tranquility. They like how far removed this place is from the everyday hubbub of their lives. But most of them don't realize the people who live around these lakes every day are hustling to scrape out a life."

He gestured to the window behind him. "Sure, there are some big businesses and some industry here in the towns along this stretch of interstate. But once you get away from town, there isn't much out there other than lakes and hills. If you don't have the credentials needed to land a job with one of the big corporations headquartered up here…there's not a lot of options."

She nodded.

"People up here are still eking out a living any way they can, like their forefathers." He thought about Harley Jenkins and how proud the man was of his granddad, the old moonshiner. "Some still farm. A few may run some cattle. Some rely on the tourism for their income."

"And working at a place like Stubby's, your sister is relying on the tourism for hers," Grace noted. "Her roommate told me Mallory makes some good tips on the weekends when the lake people are around."

Matthew nodded. "I'm sure she does. Like I said, Mallory's a pretty girl by about anybody's standards. But the tips aren't what she wants from the tourism industry," he said, his voice hardening even as the words came out.

"Oh?" Grace raised a single eyebrow. "What do you mean?"

"Mallory believes she is destined for a better life than the one she has," he explained. "It would be much easier to walk into the life she wants as opposed to earning it."

He paused. "Her main goal in life, it seems, is to meet and marry a wealthy man." He looked away from Grace's steady brown gaze. "I hate to put it so baldly," he admitted, fixating on the framed diploma hanging on his wall.

And he did hate to say so out loud. He'd worked hard to escape from the life laid out in front of him. Mallory had no idea how many late nights he'd ignored a rumbling stomach while studying, or the soul-crushing schmoozing he'd done to ingratiate himself with people who could influence his career.

He was a have-not trying to gain a toehold in the world where people had…something. But he was all too aware he'd never, no matter how hard he worked or how much money he had in his bank account, be counted as an equal to the people who had the real pull.

He knew he'd always be on the outside looking in unless someone magically handed him a golden ticket.

Mallory knew it, too.

The difference was, his sister wasn't about to work one ounce harder than she had to in order to get what she wanted. At least not the type of work that required anything more than a flirtatious smile and a willing nature.

"I don't mean to sound callous. And I'm not judging her." He gave another humorless laugh and turned back to meet Grace's eyes again. "Okay, maybe I am to a certain degree, but you have to understand, she told me all about her plans. This is the sum and total of Mallory Murray's life's ambition. She wants to marry a rich man. She wants to be taken care of. She wants everyone to envy her. She wants to be lifted out of the world she was born into."

He bit his lip and dipped his head as he drew a calming breath. At last, he forced a tired smile when he looked up again. "In a nutshell, that is the most basic thing I can tell you about my sister."

"Is it possible she's fulfilled her ambitions?" Grace asked, her gaze fixed intently on him.

Matthew fought the urge not to fidget. The detective was trying to get a read on him, but she wasn't going to find anything more than what she saw.

"It's entirely possible. Maybe she did meet the man of her dreams. Maybe they're in Las Vegas right now tying the knot. I wouldn't be surprised if she showed up with a pile of designer luggage and a rock the size of a baseball. I hope so," he added, feeling every minute of the previous night's sleeplessness. "I hope she has everything she's ever wanted. I want her to meet a guy who will treat her right, and for her to live the princess life she's always dreamed of."

"But you don't think that's the case," Grace interjected.

Matthew met her eyes again, and their gazes locked and held. "As you said earlier, we both work the same side of the law. You and I have seen how things usually pan out for young women like my sister. Tell me, how often have you seen the fairy tale come true?"

"I'm not sure I ever have," she answered with heart-stopping sincerity.

Matthew let himself slump back in his chair again and rubbed a tired hand across his forehead. "Neither have I, Grace. Neither have I."

The silence stretched between them. It seemed to go on for hours, but it was more likely seconds. At last, he heard the soft beep and lowered his hand to see she had switched off the recording. Grasping her phone, Grace leaned forward in her seat, her gaze steady on him.

"I'm going to do everything possible to find her."

He inclined his head in acknowledgment. "I'm willing to cooperate with this investigation however I can. We may not have been close, but I love my sister. I don't understand her, but I do love her."

Grace nodded, then dropped the phone into the bag at her feet. "I'm going to book a room here in town."

She extracted a business card from the outside pocket of the enormous bag she had with her and extended it to him clasped between her index and middle fingers. "My cell number is on there. Please feel free to call me if you think of anything that might be pertinent."

Matthew plucked one of his own business cards from the holder on his desk and scrawled his mobile number on the back. "You already have the office number, but same here," he replied, passing the card to her. "What's our next step?"

She let one shoulder rise and fall. "I guess there's not much more I can do until I talk to Steve. The owner of Stubby's," she added.

"Sounds logical."

She nodded. "He was the one who was working with Mallory Friday night. I'll head over there tomorrow and see what information I can get from him about where she may have gone."

He rose as she did. "I'd appreciate an update on how it goes."

"Of course," she agreed, extending her hand.

He took it, but he couldn't help feeling she was sizing him up all over again as they shook.

She cocked her head to the side. "Would you like to come out to Stubby's with me?"

He blinked and forced himself to extract his hand from hers. "Do you think it would help?"

Grace gave him a wan smile. "Can't hurt. You're familiar with the area and the people. Maybe you'd pick up on something I would miss."

Matthew found himself nodding eagerly. "Yes. Absolutely."

"When should I pick you up?" she asked.

He blinked. It hadn't occurred to him she would be the one picking him up, but he quickly chided himself for the reflexive and antiquated response. This was her investigation. He was the one riding along.

"Would eleven o'clock be too late?" He gestured to the suit he wore. "I have something at eight, and I'd like a chance to run home and change into something less conspicuous if we plan to head into the hills."

She gave a brisk nod. "Yes. Good call. Ten o'clock it is." She hiked her bag onto her shoulder and raised a hand in a half wave. "See you then."

Matthew watched as she wound her way through the maze of desks in the open area and moved toward the exit. The second the door closed behind her, he dropped back into his chair, pulled open the center drawer of his desk and stared down at the photograph he'd found in a box the previous night.

He'd removed the snapshot from the frame when they'd packed up their parents' house, but Mallory's bright smile rivaled the tiara on her head, and her eyes sparkled like the glittery tutu she wore. He rubbed a hand over his mouth.

"Lord, Mal, what the heck have you gotten yourself into now?" he asked the girl in the photo.

Chapter Five

Stubby's Bar and Grill was located on Highway 62, where it held pride of place between Beaver Lake and the more well-known Table Rock Lake, which straddled the Arkansas-Missouri state line. Not a bad location for an area heavily dependent on tourism traffic for its economy. Grace drove her state-issued SUV confidently, handling the hills and turns of the rural highway with ease.

But the man in the passenger seat wasn't relaxed, despite the fact he'd traded his courtroom suit for some more casual clothes. His slate blue flat-front chinos and a polo shirt fit him well. So well Grace had to make a point of not staring when she first saw him.

As they drove, she glanced only at his feet for the first few miles. It was safer to focus on the deck shoes he wore without socks. Those she could mock in her mind. The rest? Well, he'd been handsome but professional in his suit. But now, he looked like one of those lake people everyone kept referencing. More approachable, but still miles out of her reach.

The silence in the car might have stretched into something awkward if his phone hadn't rung before they even left town. He cast her an apologetic glance and checked the screen. "Sorry, it's the office. We've had to do some reshuffling."

"Shuffle away," she said with a wave of her hand.

The call lasted the entire stretch of road skirting north Beaver Lake. Grace was thankful for the distraction. She had debated whether to mention Kelli's discovery of the pregnancy test but decided to keep the information to herself for a bit. It was not her news to share, and until there was actual confirmation from Mallory, it was pure speculation. As a lawyer, he would understand her reticence if it came to light.

Matthew apologized again as he ended his call, but she shook her head. "No worries."

He cast a wary glance at her, and she caught a huff of a laugh. "My assistant is snowed under, and I, uh…" He trailed off, propping his elbow on the door and rubbing a hand over his mouth without continuing the thought. "I never talk much about my family. I guess they were all a little shocked when I dropped the family-emergency excuse on them."

She regarded him briefly, then turned her attention back the road. She missed the safety of his sharp suit. "It's not an excuse. It's the situation at hand."

"Right. It's… I don't take a lot of vacation. I think they all assumed I didn't have, uh, anyone." He gave a rueful chuckle. "Which, let's face it, is pretty much the gist of it."

Grace took her eyes off the road long enough to pin him with a stare. "Lots of people aren't particularly close to their family, but it doesn't mean they don't care."

"Right," he repeated, but his voice fell flat.

He shifted in his seat, and she could feel his gaze on her but resisted the temptation to meet it. "How about you? What got you into police work?"

"My grandfather was with the Fort Smith PD. I guess it's in my blood. I did my undergrad at the U of A's Fort Smith campus and was recruited by the state police from there."

"No desire to stay local?"

She smirked. "Well, technically I did. I'm based out of Fort Smith, remember?"

"Right." He hummed as he digested the tidbit. "Family still there?"

She nodded. "My mom and my older sister, Faith."

"Faith and Grace," he murmured. "No Hope?"

She raised her brows and pinned him with a stare. "Nope. My dad was a firefighter and was killed on scene. They never got any further."

"I'm sorry."

"I was barely a toddler."

"Sorry all the same," he replied.

"Thank you."

"Well, police and fire. You had your choice of footsteps to follow," he prompted.

"But working with the state is a better fit. I wanted to specialize in major crimes investigation, and the CID plays a role in most cases at one point or another. Plus, better uniforms."

"You don't wear a uniform," he pointed out.

"But I have one, and I look badass in it."

He laughed out loud. "I don't doubt it."

Grace felt heat rise on her skin. Truthfully, the slight tingle signaling the rush of blood to her ears was oddly reassuring. She thought the ability to blush had been erased from her repertoire after many years on the force.

"Thank you," she replied crisply. "How about you? Have you always wanted to be a prosecutor?"

"I only knew I wanted to be something respectable," he said, letting the words come as the thoughts formed. "I always got good grades. My mom was big on me being a doctor. Unfortunately, I'm too squeamish for medicine."

"Hard to be squeamish when you're a prosecutor," Grace pointed out. "I'm sure you've seen some pretty gruesome things."

"Yes, but usually in crime scene photographs, not live and in person."

She nodded. "Good point. Big difference."

"Absolutely." He took a breath and drummed his fingers on the armrest of the door. "It seemed like every kid I met at Fayetteville had at least one parent who is a lawyer or doctor." He snickered, and she caught him shaking his head out of the corner of her eye. "Kind of a stupid way to choose a profession, but there you go. I went to school with all these kids who were being bankrolled by doctors and lawyers, and I figured if I wasn't going to be a doctor, I might as well try to be a lawyer."

"What made you choose to serve on the side of the good guys?"

"A lot of guys I went to high school with ended up on the wrong side of the law."

He thrummed his fingers again, and she looked over to see him peering out the side window, his jaw clenched.

"Of course, they always said they were innocent,

but everybody knew they'd done whatever got them in trouble. I couldn't… I didn't think I could stomach defending somebody I knew was guilty."

"Understandable."

"Don't get me wrong—I have a lot of respect for defense attorneys. They have a tough job, and I do believe everybody deserves an advocate."

Grace couldn't stifle the derisive snort.

"Seriously. A competent defense is an absolute necessity. In order for our system of justice to work, it has to be a level playing field."

"But it's not a level playing field," she shot back, thinking of Treveon Robinson and his weeping mother. "The system is stacked against certain people—or rather, in favor of others."

"True. But I guess I thought I could do better at evening things out on the side of prosecution rather than defense."

"You're saying justice can't be served from the other side?" she challenged.

"I'm saying there's more money on the other side," he stated flatly. "And let's face it, money almost always wins. It's the American way."

They spent the rest of the drive talking about how various cases of local and regional interest had been handled, often nodding in agreement but occasionally engaging in heated debate.

Matthew pointed to a flashing roadside marquee on the left side of the highway. "Right up there."

She signaled and pulled into the cracked asphalt parking lot of Stubby's Bar and Grill. Slowing to a roll, Grace allowed herself a moment to take it all in.

The bar itself was a low cinder-block building. There didn't seem to be anything remarkable about it. The blocks had long ago been painted white but were now spattered with dirt and chipping in some spots. A portable sign with a flashing arrow had a message bragging they had the best burgers in the Ozarks, and advertised a happy hour special on bottled beer.

She crunched to a halt near the darkened double doors. The only other signage was the hand-painted lettering on the tinted glass. *Stubby's* was written in large, stylized script, and the words *Bar and Grill* were printed in a sans serif font below.

Beside her, Matthew exhaled long and loud. She turned to her passenger. Dark circles smudged his eyes. He was clean shaven, but his hair was tousled, the streaks of his fingers leaving tracks in the dark waves. His clothes were neatly pressed and stylish, but as he sat slumped in the passenger seat, she couldn't see any of the confidence he projected sitting behind his desk in the prosecuting attorney's office.

"You okay?" she asked.

He nodded. "Fine."

Grace repressed the urge to laugh at the terse response. It was clear the man was anything but fine, but she wasn't about to argue semantics with him. "I assume you've been here?"

He bobbed his head again. "Sure. Stubby's is sort of a landmark around here," he explained. "You'd be hard-pressed to find anyone who grew up in the vicinity who hadn't at least stopped in for a burger."

"Are they good?"

"Didn't you read the sign?" he asked, hooking a thumb toward the marquee. "Best burgers in the Ozarks."

"Are they?"

"I haven't done an exhaustive study, but I'd be willing to risk saying all of Carroll County."

"Is there a lot of competition for the title?"

He ducked his head, a smile curving his lips as he shook it. "Nope. At least not situated between the two lakes."

Grace had spent the previous evening studying maps of the area. The man-made lakes formed by the damming of the White River offered miles and miles of shoreline, much of it remarkably undeveloped.

"I bet those burgers and a cold beer taste good after a day out on the water."

"Nothing better," he said gruffly.

"Do you have a boat?"

He shook his head harder. "No. Maybe someday, but right now I don't have a lot of free time."

She nodded her understanding. Reaching for the door handle, she glanced over again to be sure. "You don't have to come in if you don't want to."

"No, it's good." He reached for his own door handle. "Let's go talk to Steve."

As they made their way to the plate-glass door, Grace frowned. "How familiar are you with this Steve guy?"

Matthew wobbled his hand. "Not personally. More in the way people in the area generally know other people. He's about ten years older than me. His dad was the original Stubby," he explained.

"The original Stubby, huh? There's been more than one?" she mused as he reached for the door handle.

"You'll understand the nickname when you see Steve." He paused and turned back to take in the parking area. "I don't see Mallory's car."

Grace nodded. "I didn't see one fitting the description you gave me when I came by yesterday, either."

"Interesting," he murmured as he pulled open the door.

Once inside, Grace took a moment to allow her eyes to adjust from the bright sunshine to the dim interior of the bar. There were few people in the place so early in the day. To their left, an older couple wearing golf clothes bent over baskets brimming with burgers and crinkle-cut fries. To their right, a man sagged on a stool, only his elbow keeping him upright.

Grace took a single step toward the bar, and the swinging doors she assumed led to the kitchen area pushed open. A short, squat man with a thick shock of wheat-colored hair backed through. He carried a heavy tray of what appeared to be freshly washed glasses to the bar and stowed them beneath, barely even stooping to make the task possible.

"Help you folks?" he asked without looking up.

"Yes, sir." Grace pulled her credentials from her bag and held them open for the man to inspect. "I'm Special Agent Grace Reed of the State Police Criminal Investigation Division. This is Matthew Murray from the Benton County prosecuting attorney's office."

The man's brow furrowed as he examined her identification. "Terence told me somebody came by yesterday looking for me," he said with a scowl. "What can I do for you?"

"I'm looking for information on one of your employees. Mallory Murray?"

Huffing, the short man turned away and snatched a towel from the back bar. "I told her not to bother me again. Whatever trouble she's gotten into, I'm not bailing her out. She is a good waitress, but good waitresses aren't too hard to find," he said dryly.

Grace took a step to the side, following him as he moved away from them. "We're hoping she's not in any trouble," she said earnestly. Casting a glance in Matthew's direction, she waited until he gave an almost imperceptible nod. "We wanted to ask you a few questions about Friday night."

Steve looked up from where he was wiping the bar. "Friday night?"

"Mallory Murray didn't return home Friday night and hasn't been seen since. Her roommate filed a missing-person report." She pivoted in Matthew's direction. "Mr. Murray is her brother."

The bartender looked up in surprise, his scowl deepening as he gave Matthew an unabashed once-over. "You're Mal's brother? The lawyer?"

Matthew nodded. "Yes."

Steve gave a snort. "She said you were some kind of big shot, but a person can't always pay much mind to what the girl says. Delusions of grandeur, my mama would have said," he muttered.

"We don't get to pick our siblings," Matthew retorted. "We only need to confirm she's alive and well."

"Beats me. I haven't seen your sister since she left here Friday night. If she found any trouble, it didn't happen here."

At the man's flat statement, Grace took another step toward Matthew, placing herself directly between the two men in their line of vision. "We appreciate your candor. Ms. Murray is Mr. Murray's only living family member, and I'm hoping to get some answers for him. She was scheduled to work Friday night, but we're not sure where she went from there. Do you have any idea?"

"She was scheduled, but she didn't stay long," the other man complained. "Ditched out for a party."

"Her car isn't in the parking lot," Matthew observed. "I guess she drove herself to wherever the party was?"

"I guess she did," Steve said, his expression stony.

"Any idea who might have been having this party?" Grace asked.

"The Powers kid," Steve said dismissively. "Cocky little jerk."

Grace wanted to laugh at the notion of a man she towered over by a head referring to anyone as "little," but beside her Matthew stiffened.

Pulling her notepad and pen from her bag, she flipped to a random page and scribbled the name. "Powers, you say?"

"Yeah. The young one, not his daddy," Steve clarified. "Never thought anyone would be more of a pain in the rear end than his daddy, but there you go. The rod was most definitely spared on the kid."

"Trey?" Matthew asked, his question barely more than a whisper. He cleared his throat. "You mean Trey Powers?"

Steve rolled his eyes. "Yeah, that's the one. Family has that crazy old castle over on Table Rock." His lips tightened and he shook his head. "He said something about havin' a crawfish boil that night, and she took off like a dog after a duck."

"A crawfish boil?"

"No doubt it was a catered affair," he added with a derisive snort. "Kid wouldn't know how to light his butt on fire if someone handed him a match."

The day drinker at the end of the bar barked a laugh, and Grace turned her attention to him. "You know him? This Trey Powers?" She felt Matthew go rigid again when she spoke the name, but he didn't say anything.

"You talkin' to me?" the guy at the end of the bar asked.

"I might be," she countered. "Do you know Trey Powers?"

"Everyone around here does," he replied, gesturing to the entire bar with his beer bottle.

The couple who'd been eating abruptly scraped their chairs back, dropped a twenty onto the table and rose to leave. "Thank you! Great as always," the older man called, raising a hand in farewell as he ushered his wife to the door.

Grace split a puzzled glance between Steve, his departing customers and the lawyer who'd turned into a statue beside her. "I'm sorry, how does everyone know the, uh, Powers boy?"

"You're definitely not from around here," Steve replied.

"I'm acquainted with who they are," Matthew said quietly. "You're sure she was going with him?"

"That boy and your sister have been carrying on as long as Mallory's worked here. He comes around, and she goes chasin' right after him. And that's exactly what happened Friday night." Steve tossed his towel aside in disgust. "Well, I'm done with it. When she turns up again, she doesn't need to bother coming around here wanting her job back."

Grace opened her mouth to ask more questions but stopped when she felt a hand clamp around her elbow. Glancing over at Matthew in bewilderment, she saw only his furrowed brow and the firm, forbidding line of his mouth.

"Thanks for speaking with us," he said, preemptively bringing her interview to a close. "If I see Mallory before you do, I'll be sure to pass the message along."

Grace wanted to protest, but he gave her elbow another hard squeeze. She met his eyes and found him staring back at her with eyes wide with a plea for understanding. "Let's head out, shall we, Agent Reed?"

She got the hint. He obviously knew something he didn't want to say in front of the bar owner. Pulling out a card, she slid it across the bar. "I'd appreciate a call if you hear from her."

"Yeah, sure," Steve replied.

But Grace caught sight of him chucking the card beneath the bar as Matthew all but pulled her to the tinted glass doors.

The sunlight was blinding. They stood outside the door, blinking but not speaking. At last, Matthew started to move toward her car, and she gathered her wits again.

"What was that? Who are these Powers people? How can you be so sure Steve didn't have anything more to say? I had more questions," she said, lengthening her stride to match his.

Matthew stopped beside her SUV and drew a deep

breath. "I'm giving us a chance to fall back and regroup. Trust me on this."

"Right, but—"

"Steve wasn't going to say anything helpful. The minute Mallory walked out his door, he was done with her."

"I guess we need to talk to this Trey Powers person, then," Grace persisted. "Where can we find him?"

Matthew's grim expression returned. "It's not as easy as you think." He nodded to the driver's side. "Let's go. I'll explain on the way back to town."

Grace frowned but acquiesced. She'd be a fool to discount his input. Still, the pieces weren't all fitting together for her. Opening her car door, she paused to look at Matthew.

"Should we head back to Bentonville now?" she asked across the roof of the vehicle. "Didn't Steve say they had a house on Table Rock Lake?" She hooked a thumb in the opposite direction.

"They do," Matthew confirmed. "But they don't actually live there," he added, a derisive smirk twisting his lips. "It's their lake house. The Powers family, and all that comes with them, you'll find in Bentonville."

Chapter Six

Matthew was quiet for the first few minutes of their ride back to Bentonville. Grace had to be champing at the bit to ask questions, but she remained silent as well. He appreciated her circumspection. If Mallory had taken off with Trey Powers, there would be a lot of knots to untangle.

At last, Grace cracked. "Who are these Powers people?"

"You had to have heard of some of them," Matthew insisted. "Senator William Powers?"

"This Trey guy is Senator Powers's son? I didn't think the senator had grown kids. Didn't he run on being the voice for the next generation of Arkansans? His kids are teenagers."

Matthew shook his head. "Not son, nephew." He turned to watch the passing scenery for a moment. "And yes, Senator Powers has a son from his first marriage, but he is the younger son. Tyrone Powers is the elder, and Trey's father. The family owns a law firm in Bentonville. Powers, Powers & Walton. Perhaps the other surname rings a bell?"

"Part of the Walton family?" she asked with raised eyebrows.

Matthew shrugged. "An offshoot. Close enough to be connected, but not close enough to be counting bags of money."

"You're saying these people have a lot of money and—" She halted, seeming to struggle to find an alternative to the obvious word.

"Power," Matthew provided with a wry smile. "There's no better word for it. The last couple of generations have certainly lived up to their name."

"And Trey is how old?" she asked, glancing over at him.

He shrugged again. "A couple of years younger than me, maybe?" Matthew drummed his fingers on the armrest. "He's an attorney as well, but the Powers attorneys don't bother with schools like the U of A. I think he went to Harvard. Or Yale. One of the Ivy League schools."

"Fancy," she said dryly.

"Powers, Powers & Walton is what we would consider a white-shoe law firm in this area."

"What does that mean?"

"They don't like to get dirty. They make money by protecting other people with money. Most of their cases are business related. Lawsuits, contracts, mergers and acquisitions…but every once in a while, somebody's kid gets in trouble and PP&W is there to step in."

"As defense attorneys?"

He nodded.

"I assume they're good ones."

"The best money can buy." Matthew turned to look at her. "I haven't come up against any of them in court, but people in our office have."

"Doesn't sound like confronting this Trey guy is something you're looking forward to doing."

Matthew didn't detect any judgment in her observation. "Honestly, no. There's a lot of truth in the old adage about people having the best defense money can buy."

Her mouth thinned into a disapproving line, but she nodded. "You won't get any debate on the inequities of our justice system from me."

"You see firsthand how those who don't have money suffer at the hands of our system." He fell silent for a moment. "Firms like PP&W always find a way to stack the odds in their favor. I like taking on cases I have a chance to win."

"Don't you think taking only the cases you can win is a bit ignoble?"

Her disdain came through loud and clear. "I never claimed to be noble, Agent Reed. I'm an ambitious man. I have my eye on a political career. Not only do I need to build up my résumé as a prosecutor, but I also have to be careful about who I cross. So, no, I don't want to cross swords with the Powers family."

He looked away. He didn't want to watch her expression harden. But when she spoke, her words were gentle and understanding. "I get you. Everybody has ambitions. I've spent most of my career defending mine. I'd be a hypocrite to attack you for yours."

"I'm not a fan of knocking on Trey Powers's door. I will if I have to in order to help this investigation…and my sister," Matthew said, turning to look at her. "I'm only saying I might need to tread carefully. Hell, the judge I appeared in front of yesterday used to be the

Walton in Powers, Powers & Walton. He is not my biggest fan."

"Oh?" She graced him with a smirky smile. "Contempt of court?"

"Dented his bumper," Matthew corrected.

She gasped. "Oh…my… God. I'd rather pay the contempt fine."

"I'm in judicial jail, I promise you," he said, returning her smile.

"Have you won anything in his courtroom since?"

"Of course I have," he said with a laugh. "The system is flawed, but it does work. At least, to a certain extent."

"Okay, well, don't worry, Counselor. I will handle talking to Trey Powers. No need for you to get involved."

"It won't be easy getting to him."

"I guess I'd better start my charm offensive now." He watched in a mix of amusement and horror as she initiated voice command on her phone and asked the automated assistant to call Powers, Powers & Walton in Bentonville, Arkansas.

He waited, eyebrows raised. Special Agent Grace Reed was proving to be as fearless as she was dogged. A quality that made an already attractive woman even more enticing.

A perky young receptionist answered the call. "Powers, Powers & Walton," she chirped.

"Yes, this is Special Agent Grace Reed of the Arkansas State Police Criminal Investigation Division. I need to speak to Trey Powers, please. Is he in?"

Matthew liked that she added the *please*, even though her statement wasn't remotely a request. She might be determined, but she wasn't a steamroller.

"I, uh," the young woman stammered. "Yes, ma'am." She paused, possibly realizing her tactical error. To her credit, attempted to raise the drawbridge again. "I can check. May I tell him what this is in reference to?"

"I'm afraid I can't say," Grace replied coolly.

There was another pause, then a curt, "One moment, please."

Matthew smirked. "Man, you're good," he murmured as the sound of classical piano trickled through the car's speakers.

"It's all in the delivery," she said, a smirk twitching her lips.

The two of them sat in tense silence while the piano concerto continued. Matthew would have bet money the next voice they heard was the receptionist returning to the line to tell them Trey was unavailable to take their call.

He would have lost.

Seconds later, a young male answered the phone with a mildly amused chuckle. "This is Trey Powers. May I help you?"

"Yes." Grace's grip on the steering wheel tightened, and she sat up straighter in the driver seat. "Mr. Powers, this is Special Agent Grace Reed from the Arkansas State Police Criminal Investigation Division."

"So I heard," Trey drawled, but Matthew caught the thread of annoyance that ran through each word. "What can I do for you, Miss Reed?"

Matthew swung his head to see Grace's eyes narrow, but she kept them fixed on the road ahead of them. "Agent Reed," she corrected evenly. "I'd like to set up an appointment to come in and speak to you in person, Mr. Powers."

"Concerning?"

"A young woman named Mallory Murray. I'm told the two of you are acquainted."

"Mallory Murray…" Powers repeated. "Oh, yes, Mallory. She works at Stubby's out on the highway, doesn't she?"

"Yes, sir," Grace said briskly. "Can you tell me when you last saw Ms. Murray?"

"Last saw her?" Powers asked, nonplussed. Matthew bristled at the stalling tactic. "It's been a while…"

"I'm told she left her shift at the bar to attend a party at your house last Friday evening."

"Was it last Friday? I guess so." He gave another one of those mirthless chuckles. "Sorry, it's been a long week already."

"And she was in good health when last you saw her?" Grace persisted.

There was no pause on the other end. "Absolutely. She was fine. Good health and good spirits. Beautiful as always."

"Did Miss Murray drive herself to the party at your house?" Grace asked.

"The party was not at my house here in town. It was at my family's lake house," Trey corrected, perceptibly haughtier than he'd been a few minutes ago. "And I assume she drove herself there."

"She didn't ride with you?" Grace pushed.

"Ride with me? No." The last word came out on a scoff. Matthew curled his fingers into loose fists. He wanted to introduce this cocky jerk to one of them. "No one rode with me."

"But you did invite her to come to the party at the lake house." It was a statement, not a question, but Grace's statement made it clear she expected a reply.

"I invited a number of people. It was a party. A crawfish boil. I was having it catered, so I knew there would be more than enough food," he said dismissively.

"Did you speak to Miss Murray at the party?" Grace carried on.

"Yes, we spoke," Trey answered, his words chosen with more care and spoken with deliberate measure.

Matthew sensed Grace was about to attempt to establish a more intimate connection. Trey must have felt the shift, too, because he covered the phone and spoke a few muffled words.

A second later, he said, "I'm sorry, I have a client waiting. I hope this has helped you with whatever you're investigating Mallory for, Agent Reed, but I'm afraid I have to go."

Grace didn't bother correcting his assumptions about why she was asking about Mallory, and Matthew had to admire her restraint. Agent Reed played her cards close. Nothing was given away for free. They'd confirmed a connection between his sister and Trey Powers. It would need to be enough for now.

"Thank you for speaking with me. Would it be okay if I call with any follow-up questions?" Grace asked politely.

"I'm always available to members of our law enforcement community," Trey replied, notably stiffer than he had been when the call started. "Goodbye. Good luck catching her."

A beep sounded through the speakers to signal the call had disconnected.

The hum of tires on hot tarmac filled the silence. Matthew bit his tongue, unwilling to be the one who broke peaceful contemplation. He wanted Grace's take on Trey, and for her opinions to be as untainted by his own as possible.

"Well, I guess I can say he was every bit as entitled as I expected," she commented mildly.

A snort escaped him. "Not more?"

"Well, he goes by the name Trey," she said, emphasizing the nickname by drawing the single syllable into multiples. "My expectations were pretty high."

"The Powers family is formidable," Matthew returned flatly. "You can try to talk to him again, but I'm fairly certain we just finished the last unguarded conversation you'll have with him."

Grace nodded. "I don't disagree with you."

"Where do we go from here?" Matthew asked.

"I might do some poking around online," Grace said offhandedly. "Try to get a bead on who some of the other guests were at this party. Maybe they'll have something more for us to go on. I'm not exactly sure if Mr. Powers is hedging or if he didn't pay much attention to your sister at the party."

Matthew shrugged. "Sounds like it could have gone either way. He didn't seem overly concerned about her or why anyone was asking about her."

Grace nodded. "He assumed she was in trouble. Usually when I start asking questions about someone, the first thing people ask is if they're okay. Then they start to wonder what the person I'm asking about has done wrong."

Matthew turned to gaze out the window. A sign noting the mileage back to Bentonville flew past. "I'm starting to worry," he admitted grimly.

Out of the corner of his eye, he saw her glance over at him in surprise. "Only starting?"

He sighed. "I guess I was hoping she'd taken off with some guy. Finally landed the big fish she'd been hoping to catch."

"But you don't think she has?"

Matthew unfurled his fingers and rubbed his damp palms against his thighs. "There would have been no bigger fish at that party than Trey Powers. It was his party, and he strikes me as the type who likes to be the center of attention." He closed his eyes and allowed the droning hum of tires on pavement to fill his mind for a blessed minute. "No, Mallory would not have left the party with anyone but Trey."

"It's possible he invited some other rich friends," Grace said offhandedly.

Matthew wasn't biting. "No. A Friday night crawfish boil wouldn't have been enough of an event for him to fly in Ivy League pals."

She pursed her lips as she took in his supposition. "He'd have wanted to show off something swankier."

"Exactly. I'll try to poke around at the office. Maybe someone has a friend over at PP&W we can talk to in case we can't get to Trey again." He suspected he wouldn't have much luck, but he needed to do something.

"What makes you think I can't get to him again?"

Grace asked, tapping the steering wheel in a staccato beat he could only assume was agitation.

"You won't be able to bluff and bully your way past the receptionist again," he said flatly.

"I didn't bluff or bully," she replied, indignant.

Her obvious offense brought a wry smile to his lips. "Okay, you won't be able to push your way in behind your badge."

"Says you," she muttered, casting a squinty-eyed stare his way.

"Ten bucks says they've already closed ranks," he said grimly.

"Sounds like a sucker bet," she responded on a sigh, eyes back on the road again. "Well, while you try to find an in with the suede-shoe crowd—"

"White shoe," he corrected.

"Whatever. I have a friend who specializes in tracing people online. I'll call in a favor if we can't find anything on our own, but officially, she's not supposed to look at cases unless she's assigned to them. We can take a crack at social media ourselves. After all, we're still not sure if she didn't up and take off to Vegas."

"I won't be much help to you, since I don't really use social media much, but I'll try to figure out who some of her old friends were. Maybe we can get some info from there."

"Sounds like we have our assignments," she said as they approached the Bentonville city limits. "Drop you back at the office? I assume your car is there."

Matthew checked his watch, saw it was still early afternoon, and sighed. "Yeah. I'd better go back in and see what I missed today."

Ten minutes later, Grace dropped him off in front of his office building with a promise to be in contact if she found anything of interest.

Matthew was two steps into the bustling office when Nate appeared in front of him. The prosecuting attorney gave him a slow, smirky once-over, then toasted Matthew. The paper tag attached to the tea bag in his ever-present mug fluttered with the movement. "Nice to see you again. Have we gone to casual Wednesdays now?"

Matthew shook his head, wondering how anyone could ever choose tea over coffee. "I left a message with Tracy," Matthew responded, trying not to sound defensive. "I had some business to attend to concerning my sister."

With the ease of a skilled politician, Nate assumed an expression of concerned sympathy. "I heard. Any luck?"

Matthew shook his head, not wanting to get into the nitty-gritty with his boss. Something about Nate made a person think he didn't care to be sullied with details. Matthew could never decide if this quality was ironic or not, considering Nate's job was to keep the more unsavory elements of society off the streets.

"No word yet, but Mallory has always been one to do her own thing. She could have taken off to go make jewelry in Taos."

Nate's brow beetled. "Does she make jewelry?"

Matthew shrugged. "Damned if I can tell you." He gestured toward his office. "Anyway, I figured I'd hole up in my office and spend the rest of the afternoon catching up on paperwork."

His boss dismissed him with a wave. "I was only busting your chops. Truth is, I wasn't even aware you had a sister. And I don't care if you need to sneak out and handle personal business once in a while. It's not like we've ever worked less than a ten-hour workday, right?"

Matthew had to fold his lips in and bite down to keep from refuting the statement. Nate was all about appearances. He liked to see everyone in the office—ready and raring to go.

"Right. Well, I'd better…" Matthew gestured in the direction of his office, anxious to move on.

He hated standing next to Nate in his casual clothes, even though they were perfectly acceptable office attire. As always, the prosecuting attorney was impeccably dressed. One of the inside jokes at the office was that he had each article of clothing labeled with the possibly perfect location to wear it. Striped polo shirt? Barbecue, kid's birthday party, shopping with the family. Blue blazer—informal business meetings. He didn't like casual Fridays but tolerated them because the rest of the world seemed to want them.

"Sure. Right. Back to work," Nate said with mock sternness.

Matthew tried to smile, but he never quite knew how to handle his boss. The man was a chameleon. Which was probably how he'd managed to become the youngest prosecuting attorney elected in the state. No doubt the skill had helped him make friends powerful enough to get him there.

The thought made him pause. "Hey, Nate?"

"Hmm?" The other man turned, and for a moment Matthew wondered if he'd ever seen him take a sip of tea from the mug he always held.

"Do you know Trey Powers?"

A flash of surprise crossed the other man's face, but he quickly covered it with a chuckle loaded with good humor. "Trey Powers? Of course I do. Well, I'm better acquainted with his father. Ty Powers manages a super PAC. They donated to my campaign. Why?"

Matthew made a mental note that the Powers family's political action committee was one of Nate's backers. "I guess my sister left work Friday to go to a party out at the Powers place on Table Rock Lake."

Nate nodded but looked placidly nonplussed by the information. "Ty likes to entertain out there. His father built an enormous house—looks like a European castle on the outside. All hunting lodge meets five-star ski chalet inside, of course."

Matthew couldn't contain his surprise. "You've been there?"

Nate nodded. "Most everyone who runs in political circles up here has. Since Ty's brother, Bill, decided to run for office, they got involved in all levels."

Nodding, Mathew held his ground while he digested the information. "But you've met Trey as well," he persisted.

"We've met." When he spoke, he raised and lowered one shoulder in a shrug so subtle a person who wasn't watching as intently as Matthew might have missed it. But a good prosecutor knew the value of body language, and nothing gave a person's insecurity away more quickly than a partial shrug. "He's younger. Runs with his own crowd."

"How about any of them?" he pressed. "Can you tell me who he runs around with?"

Nate frowned, but Matthew couldn't tell if it was in concentration or disapproval. "Mostly other young lawyers from PP&W. From what I hear, he didn't like being lost in a sea of other important people's kids when he went to school back East. Trey's all about being the big fish in the small pond."

"Ah."

"You're not thinking of asking Trey about your sister's whereabouts, are you?" Nate asked.

"He was the one who invited her to the party," Matthew countered. "We're hoping he can tell us where she went from there."

Nate raised his mug to his lips, blew on it, then lowered it again without taking a drink. Not meeting Matthew's gaze, he shook his head. "Listen, I understand she's your sister, and PP&W doesn't take on much criminal defense, but we don't want to get on their wrong side."

"The party was at their house."

"I understand. But Trey is the son of a man who runs a powerful firm belonging to a powerful and politically connected family. You have ambitions of your own, and I urge you to tread lightly."

"I'm not the one conducting the investigation. The state police have it."

Nate nodded. "Good. Let them do the poking and prodding."

He raised his mug in a farewell salute and turned to go back to his office. Matthew ground his molars as he made his way back to his own desk.

The thought of being told to hide behind Grace rankled, even though that had been his own instinct. But by the time he'd waved to his assistant and closed the door behind him, enough of his ire had abated for him to find humor in the vision of Special Agent Grace Reed repeatedly jabbing a bunch of Armani-clad attorneys with a single fingertip.

What Nate didn't get was the woman was more likely to employ a battering ram.

And Matthew wanted to be by her side when she used it to bust into the hallowed halls of Powers, Powers & Walton and demand to be told where his sister, Mallory, was hiding.

Chapter Seven

Grace's phone buzzed before she woke the next morning, which was never a good sign.

"Hello?" she answered, her voice husky with sleep.

"Agent Reed?" a man asked.

Grace recognized the voice instantly as her section chief, Ethan Scott. She sat up in bed. "Yes, good morning, Agent Scott," she replied, instantly more awake.

"I'm afraid it's not going to be a terribly good morning for you." He cleared his throat. "We fielded a call from some county guys this morning. A fisherman caught a body, and the general description fits one of your missing persons."

Grace closed her eyes again and braced herself. These calls were always awful, but they were particularly awful when they involved a child.

"Do they think it's Treveon Robinson?"

"No," Agent Scott answered succinctly. "I'm sorry, I should have been more specific. The call came from Carroll County. Table Rock Lake. The body fits the description of the young woman you are up there looking for...a Ms. Murray?"

Grace released a breath, but her heart rate kicked up. "Mallory Murray," she clarified.

"Yes. According to the guys on the scene, they think she's been in the water for a while. The body is bloated but recognizable. You'll need to head out there to identify and investigate the scene, but the locals tell me they doubt the area where they found her is where she went into the lake. There are no houses or cabins anywhere around there."

Grace swallowed as she nodded. "I'll head out there now. I'll also take care of notifying next of kin," she informed him.

"Jim Thompson tells me you said Ms. Murray's brother is a prosecutor up there?"

"Yes, assistant prosecuting attorney for Benton County," she reported dutifully. "His name is Matthew Murray. He accompanied me to her place of employment to ask some questions yesterday afternoon."

"Did he?"

"I had hoped having somebody who grew up in the area would encourage the owner of the bar to be more forthcoming."

Agent Scott grunted in response. Grace was trying to determine if it was approval or disapproval when he spoke. "Good thinking," he said at last. "Some of the people up in those hills don't like to talk to strangers. Particularly strangers with badges." He sighed. "The coroner is on his way and will likely beat you out there. I'll send through the GPS coordinates the county guys passed on. Apparently, this fishing hole is accessible only by a gravel road."

Of course it is, she thought wryly. As a state dependent on its natural beauty to draw tourism, Arkansas wasn't keen to pave paradise.

To her boss, she said only, "Thank you."

"Okay. Well, I guess you have your marching orders for the day. Keep me posted," he instructed.

"Yes, sir," she replied.

Ending the call, Grace sat up even straighter and tried to get her bearings. Waking up in hotel rooms was always disconcerting. Waking up to bad news in a hotel room even more so.

A peek through the crack in the blinds told her the sun hadn't been up long. She wondered for a moment if she should ask Matthew Murray if he was willing to ride along to identify the body. He'd have to do it at some point, and taking him with her now would not only slice through some jurisdictional red tape, but also would save a lot of back-and-forth driving.

It might also help them gain precious time when it came to piecing together what could have happened to his sister.

She placed the phone back on the nightstand and swung her legs over the side of the bed. True to his word, her boss sent through the coordinates. She pulled up a map and squinted at her phone, wondering how far Mallory had to stray from the Powers house to end up in those particular backwoods.

She wouldn't have answers until she got going, so Grace sprang into action. Within fifteen minutes, she was showered and dressed in jeans and a T-shirt with the State Police logo on the front and *CID* across the back in block letters. After scraping her hair back into a low ponytail, she returned to the bed, where she sat down to put on her shoes. Like the ponytail, they were serviceable—scuffed black oxfords she wore more for comfort than style.

Once she was put together, she picked up her phone and cradled it in her hands, an internal war waging.

She knew nothing yet. It could have been an accident. Mallory could have gotten drunk and stumbled away from the party and into the lake. If there were enough guests, it was entirely possible no one noticed the waitress from the local burger joint wandering away.

A remote inlet with no houses nearby.

There were hundreds if not thousands of nooks and crannies in the lake's shoreline. Large parcels of undeveloped land. There would be wide swaths of area to search. There was nothing to say she'd been anywhere near the Powers family home when she ended up in the water. Heck, someone could have boosted the car, killed her and dumped her body in the lake.

Grace sighed and pulled up Matthew Murray's contact information, still not sure asking him to ride along was a good idea or not. There were too many scenarios, and she didn't have enough answers. But something told her she needed to give Matthew the option of seeing the scene.

She shook her head, refusing to overthink the day away. Her jaw set in agitation, she made the call. Matthew was a grown man. He could decide what was best for him.

Murray sounded far more awake than she expected when he answered with a brisk "Agent Reed?"

"Good morning," she greeted automatically. Then

she closed her eyes on a wince. "Well, I'm sorry. It's not a good morning," she corrected herself.

"I take it you have some news on Mallory," he said flatly.

"A fisherman found a body in one of the inlets on Table Rock Lake. The county deputies on scene are fairly certain they have a match."

Matthew's sharp inhale of breath sounded tangled in his throat. And she felt her own constrict with sympathy.

"Where?"

"They found her in a pretty undeveloped area. No houses nearby." In answer to his unspoken question, she added, "I'm not sure exactly how far away it is from the Powers family lake house. All I have are GPS coordinates."

She heard another ragged rush of breath.

"I'm sorry," she added. "I haven't been out there to confirm as of yet. Right now, the county is handling things, but I'll need to canvass the scene and make an initial identification."

He didn't bother clearing the rasp from his throat. "I understand."

"I'm heading out there now. I can keep you informed as I—"

"I want to go with you," he interjected.

"I thought you might. Listen, you see a lot of things in your line of work—" she began.

"We both do," he interrupted again. "I'm aware of what to expect."

Or he thought he did. But he wouldn't be looking at photographs of a stranger. "If you come with me to identify, it would save us a step."

"Do you want me to meet you out there?"

Grace thought about it for a moment. It would be easier not to have the victim's brother in tow while she went over the scene, but the county guys probably knew best in this case. There likely wouldn't be much evidence to collect. Plus, the thought of asking him to drive those winding, hilly roads alone after receiving word that the last member of his family might be dead seemed cruel. He and his sister may not have been close, but she was all he had.

"I could pick you up if you'd like," she offered.

There was silence on the other end of the line. She assumed he was weighing the pros and cons as well.

At last, he said only, "I'll text you my address."

"On my way shortly."

Grace gathered the bag containing her evidence kit and her ASP windbreaker and headed for the door. She turned the radio off for the drive to Matthew Murray's place. She didn't have the patience for morning drive chatter.

To her surprise, Matthew didn't live in one of the thousands of new-construction condominiums littering the I-49 corridor, but rather in a bungalow on the south side of the old downtown Bentonville. She realized as she pulled up to the curb in front of the address that he was likely walking, or at least biking, distance from his office. Again, she suffered a bout of commute envy. She was about to text to let him know she was outside when the front door opened.

Matthew came out dressed in jeans and a University of Arkansas T-shirt. He wore hiking boots and carried a zippered hoodie in one hand. This was a man who was clearly accustomed to the terrain. Grace glanced down at her own shoes and hoped the sturdy soles would be up to the task.

Two aluminum travel cups were cradled in the crook of his arm. Matthew slid into the passenger seat, and the scent of freshly brewed coffee filled the air. Without asking, he offered her one of the cups. She gave him a wan smile. "I appreciate the thought, but I'm not a coffee drinker."

"Philistine," he said in a gruff whisper. "More for me."

"There's the upside," she said. Lifting her refillable water bottle from the cup holder, she took a swig. "I'm all about the hydration."

"Water is overrated." Matthew placed a travel mug in the other cup holder and took a deep swallow from the one he still held.

Grace slowed at a stop sign. Glancing over at him, she asked, "How are you holding up?"

"I'm trying not to dwell on it too much," he replied, turning to look out the passenger window. "Seems unreal."

"I understand."

And she did. Having lost her father at a young age, Grace understood what it was to mourn somebody even if you hadn't been particularly close. Thankfully, her relationship with her mother and her sister made up for the gap in her life. But Matthew wouldn't have anyone.

Hoping to keep her focus on the task at hand, she tapped the map displayed on the in-dash GPS. "Are you familiar at all with the area?"

"I'm familiar with most of it, but Table Rock has a lot of fingers. Tons of inlets and private roads."

"I'd like to get some information on where the Powers family's lake house is located. You have any sources who might be able to dig it up?" Matthew nodded, but she sensed hesitation in the movement. "Unless asking creates an uncomfortable situation for you."

He pulled a grimace. "My boss is pretty well acquainted with the family, but I don't want to ask him. He made it clear I should avoid poking the bear if I value my future."

Her eyebrows shot up. "Did he? He flat out told you not to talk to Trey Powers?"

Matthew chuckled. "We're attorneys. We don't flat out tell anyone anything." He drummed his fingers on his thigh. "But I got the message."

"I see."

"I could probably do some back-channel asking around, though," he said quietly. "Shouldn't be too hard to figure out. Property records are public."

"Yeah, but public records can be tricky. It might be held in a trust or something."

He nodded. "It gets complicated when a family has too much money." She glanced over at him. "I doubt it's held in only one person's name."

She frowned as she digested the information. "Right."

"Most have some kind of umbrella company with a name not obviously connected to them," he said distractedly. "Makes it easier to squeeze big chunks of property through the tax loopholes."

"No doubt."

"Any luck on the social media front?" he asked.

"I didn't get far in." She turned right onto the highway, as the navigation system directed. "I did go onto the law firm's website and took note of a few names of the younger associates. I figured they'd be more apt to post photos and other information on social media. There are headshots, too."

He nodded. "Good thinking."

"I haven't found much. A lot of people use only their first and middle names or nicknames as a way to keep employers from snooping around, but I did find a couple of people who posted pictures from a Christmas party the firm held last year. They tagged some of the other attorneys, but nothing pointed directly to this party at the lake."

"I'll see if my assistant, Tracy, can dig up some names of the paralegals or assistants over there," he told her, pulling his phone from his back pocket. "They may not be as paranoid as the attorneys themselves. It's not a big community. She may be able to poke around and possibly get some leads on people to talk to."

They rode in silence as he tapped out a couple of text messages.

Grace got the feeling he didn't want to talk much, which was a relief, because she was at a loss for what to say next. She reached for the car radio. "Music?"

"Please," he answered as he typed out another text.

After searching around a bit, she settled on a classic rock station but kept the volume low. They exchanged few words until the GPS directed them to turn off the two-lane road and onto a rutted lane of dirt and gravel.

The bumpy road jostled them around for a good minute.

"Sorry, I'm trying to go slow," she said, dividing a glance between him and the narrow lane. "This is pretty bad."

"Most of them are like this. Not enough money in

the county to keep them up regularly. Plus, you get a lot of people on ATVs and dirt bikes out here tearing them up."

"Makes sense." She gave a soft "Oof" as they hit a particularly rough patch.

The road sloped sharply downhill. She checked the screen on the dash and determined they must be close to the shoreline, judging by the amount of blue water showing on the navigation. Sure enough, they came around another curve and spotted a handful of county vehicles clustered around an old two-tone pickup truck.

"This must be the place," he said grimly.

She pulled to a stop behind the van marked Coroner and turned to look at him. "You sure you're okay to do this here? I don't mind if you want to wait until they have her cleaned up a bit."

Matthew shook his head. "No. There's no sense in putting it off." He reached for the door handle. "I need to see for myself if it's her."

Grace nodded, killed the engine and reached for her jacket. Climbing out of the car, she said only, "Let's go."

The men gathered at the back of the coroner's van straightened as they approached.

"Deputy Carson?" Grace called out to the two uniformed men.

A tall, barrel-chested man with a stomach determined to test his shirt buttons stepped forward. "I'm Jeff Carson."

"Grace Reed, ASP CID," she said, extending her hand.

They shook, and he turned to the other men assembled. "This here is Deputy White," he said, indicating the other uniformed officer. "Mr. Nelson is the county coroner." He nodded to a man beside the other deputy, then he placed a hand on the shoulder an ashen-faced older man dressed in baggy cargo shorts and a well-worn T-shirt advertising a cigarette brand. "This is Willard Johnston. He's the one who found her."

Grace took each of their proffered hands in turn, then gestured to Matthew. "This is Matthew Murray. We believe the victim may be his sister. He's here to help us with identification," she said, directing the last to the coroner.

Nelson nodded. "We are fairly certain, judging from the photograph you have on file, but if you'll follow me."

She and Matthew trailed Nelson to the back of the van, where the double doors stood open. The other men did not follow. Grace could only assume they had seen enough for one day.

"I don't mind taking her in and, uh, making her more, uh, presentable," he said, casting a wary glance at Matthew.

"Mr. Murray is a prosecuting attorney for Benton County. He has seen bodies before."

Nelson hesitated, his hand on the zipper of the body bag. "All due respect, Mr. Murray, seeing a body pulled right out of the water and looking at a postmortem photo are totally different. It's rough, even when the victim is not kin."

"I understand," Matthew assured him, but his voice was hoarse. "It's okay."

The coroner nodded his understanding. "All right, then."

Nelson pulled his phone from his pocket, opened a voice-recording app and unzipped the bag about eighteen inches. He spoke the date, time and their approximate location into the phone, then parted the fabric.

"Mr. Murray, can you identify the body of this young woman?"

Matthew swallowed hard as he stared down at the water-bloated face, and empathy welled up inside Grace. No matter how often she had to witness the worst moments in a person's life, she'd never grown inured to them. She hoped she never would.

Grace put a steadying hand on his arm when he simply nodded. "We'll need you to give a verbal answer, if you can," she prompted gently.

"Yes," he croaked. "Yes, this is my sister." The last word caught on a sob.

"Her name?" she whispered, giving his arm a reassuring squeeze.

"Mallory," he managed to say in a strangled voice. "Mallory Murray."

With a heaving gasp, Matthew tore himself from her grasp and emptied the contents of his stomach into the trampled grass.

Chapter Eight

Grace climbed into the SUV and found Matthew grim-faced and firing off message after message on his phone. It chimed incessantly. His thumbs flew as she stowed her bag and slid into the driver's seat. Matthew didn't look up from the screen.

He didn't ask any questions—which she found particularly odd, considering his occupation and the personal connection—but she figured maybe he was embarrassed to have lost his coffee in the weeds. Three more messages had arrived before she hit the ignition. He answered them in quick succession.

Unnerved by the brittle air of hyperconcentration emanating from him, she felt compelled to break the silence.

"Nelson's first impression isn't drowning."

His head snapped back as if she'd punched him. She met his gaze directly, confident she now had his full attention. The phone in his lap dinged and dinged, but Matthew didn't look away.

"Based on what?" he asked.

It was a nonsensical question coming from a prosecutor, but Grace was glad she'd jolted him back into brother mode with the direct approach. She spoke quietly but with conviction.

"She sustained a blow to the head."

"Could have happened after she was in the water. Maybe she hit a submerged log and it knocked her unconscious."

The coroner had given her the usual spiel about not being certain until they were able to autopsy the body, but they were both professionals and had seen enough to draw some fairly strong initial conclusions.

"You're right. We have to wait for the postmortem," she conceded.

"But you think she was struck prior to going in the water."

"Pure conjecture," she admitted. The image of a positive pregnancy test flashed in her mind's eye.

They hadn't found anything in the pockets of the shorts Mallory had been wearing, but she might have left the other test in her car… Had she mentioned the pregnancy to Matthew? Should Grace say something now?

She decided to wait awhile longer. If their preliminary conclusions played out, an unwanted pregnancy could be a strong reason to give Trey Powers a good, long look. Assuming he was indeed the father.

Right now, all they had was a lot of supposition and not much evidence.

"The county deputies can't determine whether any of the items they've recovered from the scene might be evidence or if they're nothing more than trash washed up on the shore, but they bagged whatever they could find."

Grace instantly regretted the words she'd just spoken.

This man's sister had washed up on the same shoreline, like someone's discarded goods. She wasn't working at her highest level at the moment. Determined to put things right, she cranked the wheel and began to make the tight back-and-forth turns to get them on the path headed out.

Matthew turned his head toward the lakeshore. "It could have happened anywhere out there."

"You're right. And I am sorry for your loss," Grace said quietly. "You two weren't close, but it doesn't make it any easier."

"Thank you," he answered gravely. He grunted as one wheel dropped into a hole in the sad excuse for a road. "While I was waiting, I was thinking…maybe we could swing back by Stubby's."

"Stubby's? Sure, but why?" she asked as she cranked the wheel and pointed the nose of the SUV in the direction of the highway.

"I was thinking we could show Steve some of the photos of the associates on the PP&W website. He might recognize some of them if they were with Trey Friday night."

A startled laugh popped out of her, and Grace turned to look at him instantly sheepish. "Sorry. I can't believe I didn't think of asking him myself."

"It may not give us anything, but I have to feel like I'm doing something."

"I understand." With cautious efficiency, she wove her way between the ruts and potholes, moving as quickly as she could without jarring them too much. "If what you say about PP&W is true, it may be easier to get to some of the other people who work there than Trey Powers himself."

"Exactly."

They bumped along in silence for a minute. "I made a few calls and, with Nelson's agreement, arranged for the coroner to transfer your sister to the Benton County coroner's facilities. They have a decent forensics lab there, and I figured you would prefer to have the initial postmortem handled locally. They will have to work with the state crime lab, though."

"Thank you, I appreciate the thought," he said with a slow nod. "Sorry again for…" He hooked a thumb over his shoulder but let the words trail away.

"No need to be sorry. I've seen twenty-year veterans lose their lunch on scenes. It may or may not have happened to me as well," she added with a wry smile.

He looked over at her. "You can neither confirm nor deny?"

"Precisely."

"I understand."

When they finally hit the opening onto the paved county road, she slowed to a stop to be sure there was no oncoming traffic. No one. This was a weekday, and the county guys hadn't been wrong about the lack of development. The only reason Mr. Johnston had gone down there to fish was that it had been the spot where his own father had taken him as a boy.

She and Mathew exchanged a glance. In silent accord, she turned left, away from town and in the direction of Stubby's Bar and Grill.

"Any luck with your assistant?" she asked, nodding to the phone in his hands.

"No, not much," he said grimly. "Mostly, I've been going back and forth with Nate, lining out the cases I'm working on. Someone can step in for the next few days while I handle whatever arrangements need to be handled."

"Nate is the prosecuting attorney?"

Matthew nodded. "He's a nice guy. Mostly. Ambitious." He turned the word over in his head. "I guess it figures. He did his undergraduate at the U of A but went to Yale Law, so he has a foot in both worlds."

"I see."

"Anyway, we were trying to sort out what loose ends I might have."

"It'll be a few days until they can release her body."

He nodded. "Yeah, but I figure I'll need to get whatever she had at the apartment cleared out, get a handle on the state of her bills, bank accounts and other stuff."

Grace nodded, thinking of how sad it was that the remains of someone's life could be boiled down to the word *stuff*. She did not allow herself to give in to the pang of guilt when he mentioned going to the apartment in Eureka Springs. She wouldn't ask Mallory's roommate to keep the pregnancy test a secret, but she still wasn't sure she would tell Matthew about it. Yet.

She needed to put a few more puzzle pieces together first.

"OH, YEAH, SHE was definitely one," Steve said, jabbing a blunt finger at the screen of Grace's phone. "Looked even younger in person. I carded her."

"Did you?" Grace asked, mildly surprised to discover anyone was ever carded at Stubby's.

He squinted at the screen, nodding more emphatically. "She's wearin' makeup and a stuffy suit here, so she looks older, but the other day she was all freckled and had her hair in two braids like my nieces used to wear. Looked about twelve."

"You're certain Taylor Greene was in here the day Mallory took off to go to the party at the Powerses' place?" Matthew reiterated.

Steve shrugged. "If that's her name, yeah."

Grace waited as Matthew tapped out a note on his phone. A ballgame was showing on one of the bar's televisions, but the barfly who'd been there the previous day sat perched on the same stool watching what appeared to be a soap opera.

Dragging her attention away from the couple in a heated argument on the screen, she redoubled her efforts on getting information out of Steve. "And you think you possibly remember Joshua Potter," she pushed, thumbing through the headshots they'd swiped from the website until she landed on one of a man with a receding hairline and tortoiseshell glasses.

"Not as sure about him, but I remember a guy with glasses." Steve took a step back from the bar, twisting the towel he'd balled in one hand into a long rope. "Not as bad as the other guy. Obnoxious jerk. He actually snapped his fingers at me. Who does that in real life?" he asked, incredulous.

"Obnoxious jerks," Matthew murmured as he typed a note into his own phone.

"Exactly," Steve said, pointing at Matthew. "You think maybe Mal has taken off with one of these two? Or is it some kind of love-triangle thing?" Steve settled a hip against the cooler below the bar and crossed his short arms over his broad chest. "Gotta be honest, I never pegged Mallory for the type to get in the middle of something. The girl pretty much wanted what she wanted, and she wanted it all to herself, if you get what I'm saying."

Matthew looked up, clearly startled by the man's astute observation.

Grace stepped in. She didn't want either of them wandering too far down the path of extolling Mallory's myriad shortcomings. The woman may not have been anyone's idea of dependable, or even maybe trustworthy, while she was among them, but she didn't deserve to be dragged through the mud in death.

"No, we're no longer looking for Ms. Murray," she interjected smoothly.

Steve shook his head in confusion. He glanced at Matthew before letting his questioning gaze land on her again. "Not looking for her? What's this all about, then?"

"We're simply trying to determine who all may have been attending the party at the Powers house Friday night," she replied evenly.

"Yesterday you were in here asking questions about Mallory because you couldn't find her." He directed this at Matthew. "Now you tell me you're not looking for her anymore, but you still wanna come in here asking questions?"

The day drinker let out a derisive snort. "Some people need to mind their own damn business," he grumbled to no one in particular.

"It *is* my business," Matthew snapped. "She was my sister."

An uneasy silence filled the barroom as his use of the past tense in regard to Mallory settled over them like a shroud.

"Was?" Steve repeated blankly. He looked truly stricken, all the tough words he'd had for Mallory forgotten as the color drained from his florid face. "Mal's not… She's okay, isn't she? I mean, you're not looking for her anymore… You found her?"

Grace exhaled in a soft whoosh as Matthew dropped his gaze to the sticky floor. She spoke directly to Steve, low and confidential. "I'm afraid Ms. Murray's body was found this morning."

"Found?"

"A fisherman found her body," she said, keeping the details as sparse as she could while still conveying the gravity of the situation.

"A fisherman? Who? Where?"

"Table Rock," Matthew answered, dropping the words like wet sandbags between them with a thud.

Steve was quick on the uptake. His narrowing gaze flew to Matthew, then back to the phone in her hand. "And you're here askin' about all those lawyers because…" He snapped his jaw shut. "Holy Moses—"

He scraped a hand over his face, pulling on his jowls as he spun away from them. She could see his reflection in the mirror behind the bottles lining the back bar. He looked horrified.

And scared.

She saw his mouth move, but his voice was barely

more than a whisper. "You think the Powers kid was involved."

"We have no evidence of foul play," Grace stated, enunciating each word with great care.

"No," Steve said as he turned back to her. "But you think he is."

"Since he was hosting the party, we are certainly interested in speaking with Mr. Powers. I would be interested in speaking to anybody who came in contact with Mallory after she left here last Friday evening. As I said, we have nothing concrete. We believe Ms. Murray perished between Friday evening, when she left here at about…" She trailed off, raising her eyebrows in a prompt.

Steve shrugged. "Around six thirty or seven, maybe? The dinner crowd had cleared out for the most part, but the lake people and the evening drinkers were starting to come in."

Grace nodded. "Right. Between seven o'clock Friday evening and five o'clock this morning, something happened to Mallory Murray. It's my job to piece together what those events may have been."

Steve shook his head. "I can't tell you anything more."

"And we appreciate your input," Grace said smoothly. "We wouldn't be bothering you again, except it occurred to us you might be able to help us identify who some of the other people in Mr. Powers's party might have been."

"I can't swear to any of it," Steve hastened to add. "Well…maybe the girl, but I didn't pay much attention to the group of them. I see a lot of people in a day. People from all walks of life. Unless you're a local, I don't pay much mind. No point in getting too into it with people who are breezing through, right?"

"Absolutely. No point in getting too involved."

Steve shifted his attention to Matthew, who'd switched off his phone and dropped it into his pocket. "I'm awful sorry about Mallory," the bartender said. "I was kind of a jerk about her yesterday, but I did like the girl. She was one of the best I'd ever had working here. God's honest truth."

"I appreciate you saying so," Matthew replied, offering Steve his hand to shake. "And trust me, I am well aware how frustrating Mallory could be. I don't blame you for getting teed off at her. She gets under my skin pretty regularly." He paused. "Got. She got under my skin pretty regularly," he repeated, his expression grim as he switched tenses.

Steve wrung the bar towel again. "I am sorry."

Grace pulled another of her business cards from her pocket and slid it across the bar as she had on her first visit. "If you think of anything else. Anything at all. Even if you think it isn't important, please feel free to call me. All my numbers are on the card."

Steve picked up her card and slid it into the back pocket of his jeans rather than tossing it under the bar. "I will. I promise."

Matthew nodded. "Appreciate your help."

They turned to go. As they reached the door, Steve called out to them again. "Will you keep me posted? About any arrangements?"

Matthew looked back at the other man, clearly startled by the request. "Arrangements?"

Steve gave them helpless shrug. "I'd send flowers or something."

Matthew bowed his head, but when he lifted it he said, "I appreciate the thought. Not sure what I'm going to do, but save the flower money. If you want do something, make a donation to a worthy cause. Anything you think Mallory would like," he suggested. "After all, you probably knew her better than I did."

Steve nodded and gave a mirthless chuckle. "I knew her well enough to tell you there wasn't a cause she thought was more worthy than her own."

Matthew smiled at the comment, touching the end of his nose to indicate the accuracy of the other man's statement. "You hit the nail on the head there. Throw a party here for her one night. She'd have liked a party."

"Will do," Steve assured him. "I'll call if I think of anything else."

"Appreciate you." Grace raised a hand in farewell.

They stepped out of the dimly lit bar into the bright summer morning.

"I hope you don't mind that I told him," Grace said quickly. "I figured he was her employer and would have to be told eventually, and this way at least we could use the shock value to garner what information we could."

"No." He gave her a tired smile. "I don't mind."

He paused at the passenger door and looked back at the cinder-block building. "Well played, Agent Reed. What's our next move?"

She gave it a moment of thought. "Well, I think our next move is to head back to town. I'll need to call Kelli Simon and let her know Mallory has been found. You'll need to wait for the coroner's report to be complete before you can make arrangements, and I need figure out how to get in to see Trey Powers and friends."

"Easier said than done."

"Don't you worry, I have my ways," Grace answered with a confidence she didn't feel. But she'd make things happen; she always did. Clicking the key fob to unlock the doors, she said, "Saddle up, Counselor. I think this ride's about to get a whole lot more interesting."

Chapter Nine

Tom Petty hadn't lied when he said the waiting was the hardest part, but Matthew wasn't simply sitting around waiting for his phone to ring. Not when he knew deep in his gut a privileged coward like Trey Powers was involved in his sister's death. He didn't care if Powers's involvement was accidental or deliberate. At this point, intent didn't matter. If Trey had any inkling of Mallory falling into the water, he was at least an accessory after the fact.

Sitting in his sparsely furnished living room, he scrolled through Mallory's PicturSpam account. Again. But his sister hadn't posted any photos last Friday night. Nor were there any of her with Trey. The closest he'd come was a selfie she'd taken with another woman about her age. Her companion was a toothy blonde. They both had eyelashes too dark and thick to be natural and held tall hurricane glasses filled with a liquid so virulently green Matthew couldn't believe anyone would willingly ingest it.

He'd looked at the same picture at least a half dozen times in the days since Agent Reed told him Mallory had disappeared, and he hadn't noticed anything out of the ordinary. But now, after two trips to Stubby's and one truncated phone call with the cocksure princeling, he finally figured out why he kept coming back to it again and again.

A watch.

In the photo, a man's arm lay draped casually across his sister's shoulders. A man who apparently had breath-takingly expensive taste in wristwatches.

The oversize face of the watch was visible thanks to the casual drape of his arm. He'd had a roommate in law school who was obsessed with collecting watches, so Matthew knew they were as much of a status symbol for some men as diamonds or designer handbags were for some women. Matthew recognized the hallmark of a prestigious brand below the diamond at the top of the bright blue dial.

A few quick queries helped him pin it down. Whoever was staking his claim on Mallory had been wearing a Poseidon. Another search revealed the watch hadn't been available for sale at any jeweler in Arkansas. It was an exclusive model, and the nearest retailers with access were in Dallas, Kansas City or Baton Rouge.

There was a lot of money in the northwest corridor of Arkansas, but not many young people with the kind of money they could blow on spendy jewelry.

Most didn't bother. The area was rife with avid hikers or sportsmen. They'd go for a model with some sort of GPS rather than throw down for a blue sunburst face and a bunch of analog dials.

Matthew glanced at his own smart watch. He'd been leery of dropping a few hundred dollars on the latest model when it became available, but looking at the price tags attached to the man bling on the website, he felt far more secure in his frugal life choices.

"Pays to be oblivious," he muttered, tapping an icon on the display of the decidedly less prestigious watch he wore. "Call Grace Reed on mobile."

The automated assistant put the call through.

"Can't sleep?" Grace asked by way of greeting.

"I'm sorry," he grimaced, noticing the hour. It was after midnight. "Were you sleeping?"

"Nah. I'm a night owl," she assured him.

Since she sounded fully awake and alert, he took her at her word. "Hey, I came across something. Could be nothing, I'm not sure…"

"Hit me," she prompted.

"Can you pull up Mal's PicturSpam feed? I want you to look closer at one of the pictures."

He heard her tapping. "Okay. Which one am I looking for?"

"Fourth or fifth picture down, there's one of Mallory and another girl holding some nasty-looking green cocktails. See it?"

"Yup. Wouldn't drink one on a bet, though."

"Me, either." Matthew smiled, enjoying the moment of synchronicity in what was an otherwise surreal day. "A guy has his arm around Mal's shoulders. Can you zoom in on his watch?"

"His watch?" she repeated, not bothering to mask her puzzlement.

"Yeah."

A beat passed, and then she said, "Nice watch. Silver with a blue face, lots of dials."

"Do you see the brand symbol?"

"No," she said, drawing the words out. "Not really. Is it some kind of upside-down *T* or something?"

"An anchor."

"Oh. Yeah, okay, I see it now." She paused. "What about it?"

He tried to formulate how he might explain. "Okay, this is going to sound weird…probably because it *is* weird to many mere mortals, but some guys have a thing for watches."

"You didn't call me at midnight to confess some weird watch fetish, did you?"

"Not at all," he hastened to assure her. "But anyway, the guy I roomed with while I was in law school? He was one of those guys. Used to get jazzed about them. Like, he has a whole plan for which watches he would collect on his way to attaining his dream watch."

"O-kay," she drawled, clearly perplexed. "Are you trying to tell me you think your old roommate is in this picture?"

"No. He's in Los Angeles working his way up to a junior partnership at a firm specializing in entertainment law."

"And he wants this watch…"

"It's a Poseidon."

"And that's…good?"

"Well, I'm not sure where it ranks on my friend's sliding scale now, but this watch would come in at about one or two steps higher than his dream watch."

"Seriously?"

She sounded incredulous, and Matthew couldn't blame her. He felt pretty much the same.

"Yeah. Mike had his sights set on a stainless steel

model, but judging by the dials and what I see on the website, I think this one might be white gold."

He sent her the link to the brand site. "Look under the Elite collection."

A minute later, Grace gave a low whistle. "Holy cow."

"No doubt," he said gravely.

"And you can get matching cuff links, if you feel like you need something extra after spending on a watch what most people would spend on a house," she said, her voice rising with her agitation.

"Rich people," he said in a flat, derisive voice.

GRACE LAUGHED. The sheer ridiculousness of spending tens of thousands of dollars on something that didn't provide food, shelter or any other basic necessity demanded she laugh. Matthew laughed, too, and she instantly felt better. The man had seen his only family member zipped into a body bag hours ago, but he still could find humor in life's absurdities. She supposed it was something cops and prosecutors had in common.

As their chuckles quieted, she sighed. "Of course, I don't have to tell you this isn't evidence of any connection between your sister and Trey Powers."

"No, you don't," he said, resigned.

The silence hummed between them, but it felt oddly comfortable to Grace. A full minute must have passed before he spoke again.

"What do you do when you can't sleep?"

The chuckle that escaped her was mirthless. "Work."

"I can't concentrate," he confessed.

"Totally understandable. You've suffered a loss.

You're grieving. It's not your job to concentrate right now—it's mine."

"I can't sit around waiting for something to happen."

While Grace understood the sentiment entirely, she needed to put him gently but firmly in his place. "I totally get you, but now your focus needs to be on Mallory. My focus will be on making sure anyone who may have been involved in her death is brought to justice."

"I thought we played on the same side." His reminder came out stiff and somewhat belligerent.

Grace could see how such stubbornness would serve him well as a prosecutor. "We are on the same side, but you're not the prosecutor, you're the brother." She waited a beat to let her admonishment sink in. But Matthew's response was not the escalation of agitation she anticipated.

"What if I can't be the brother she needs?" he asked at last. "I haven't been a good one up to this point, and it looks like I won't have any more chances."

"But you do," she reminded him, her voice gentle. "Mallory still needs you. Now more than ever. It might not be in the way either of you would have chosen, but the fact of the matter is you're all she has."

"And you," he said gruffly.

"Absolutely."

A pang of guilt twisted in her gut. She remembered the day she took the call from Mallory's roommate and how annoyed she'd been to be distracted from the case she'd deemed more worthy than the disappearance of a flighty party girl.

Grace knew all too well the chances of finding Treveon alive grew slimmer by the day, but whether her victims needed her in life or in death didn't matter. Like Treveon, Mallory would be counting on her to unravel the story.

"Usually when I can't sleep, I like to spend hours dwelling on the cases where I failed a victim and what I would have done differently," she confessed.

"And it helps you sleep?" he sounded incredulous.

"No. Never. But it fuels me. I am the one these people are counting on. It's what gives me the push I need to try harder, do better, be faster." She stopped there and swallowed hard. "I'm sorry I didn't get there fast enough for Mallory."

"You got there as fast as you could," he said gently. "You did. I have a gut feeling you're not going to allow Mallory's death to linger on your list of regrets."

"You and your gut don't know me at all, Counselor," she said, her voice husky with emotion.

"I've seen enough over the past couple of days," he reassured her. "I'm confident this will not be a case you'll lay awake replaying in your mind."

"I'm supposed to be comforting you," she reminded him.

Matthew chuckled. "Oddly enough, I do feel better."

"You start working on the things you need to do for Mallory. I'll call or text you as soon as I have any information from the coroner."

"And if it comes out it's more than an accident, you'll keep me up-to-date on any further investigation into any, uh, suspects?" he pushed.

"I don't believe this is going to fall under your jurisdiction," she reminded him.

More to Love.
More to Explore.

With more to explore, we'd love to send you up to 4 BOOKS, absolutely FREE when you try the Harlequin Reader Service.

They say that "less is more" — but not when it comes to reading your favorite books!

We know that readers like you can't wait to open their newest book and settle down reading.

We feel the same way. That's why today, you can say "YES" to MORE of the great reading you love — absolutely FREE!

Try **Harlequin® Romantic Suspense** books featuring heart-racing page-turners with unexpected plot twists and irresistible chemistry that will keep you guessing to the very end.

Try **Harlequin Intrigue® Larger-Print** books featuring action-packed stories that will keep you on the edge of your seat. Solve the crime and deliver justice at all costs.

Or **TRY BOTH** and get 2 books from each series!

Your free books are completely free, even the shipping! If you continue with your subscription, you can look forward to curated monthly shipments of brand-new books from your selected series, always at a discount off the cover price! Plus you can cancel any time.

So don't miss out, return your Free Books Claim Card today to get your Free books.

Pam Powers

Free Books Claim Card
Say "Yes" to More Books!

◀ DETACH AND MAIL CARD TODAY! ▼

YES! I love reading, please send me more books from the series I'd like to explore and a free gift from each series I select.
Get MORE to read, MORE to love, MORE to explore!
Just write in "**YES**" on the dotted line below then select your series and return this Claim Card today and we'll send your free books & gift asap!

➡ _YES_ ⬅

Which do you prefer?

☐ **Harlequin® Romantic Suspense**
240/340 HDL GRSA

☐ **Harlequin Intrigue® Larger-Print**
199/399 HDL GRSA

☐ **BOTH**
240/340 & 199/399
HDL GRSX

FIRST NAME	LAST NAME

ADDRESS

APT.#	CITY

STATE/PROV.	ZIP/POSTAL CODE

EMAIL ☐ Please check this box if you would like to receive newsletters and promotional emails from Harlequin Enterprises ULC and its affiliates. You can unsubscribe anytime.

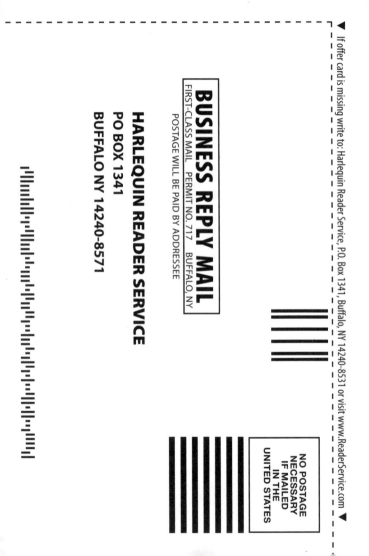

"Please," he added. "The only way I can help her now is by helping you. Let me do whatever I can do."

Grace let silence stretch between them for a minute. "I'll be in touch, Mr. Murray. Try to get some sleep."

"You, too, Agent Reed. And thank you."

GRACE DID GET some sleep, but not a lot. After she ended the call with Matthew, she'd spent precious hours thinking about the stupid wristwatch he'd been worked up over. She couldn't imagine a world in which people paid insane money for a watch, but as Matthew pointed out, even among the wealthy there weren't many who could. Folks she would have considered well-off weren't in the same league as someone who could spend that kind of money on a piece of jewelry simply because they wanted it.

A morning spent researching the Powers family confirmed they had indeed reached an unfathomable level of wealthy. The original Tyrone Powers started accumulating the family fortune while working in the lumber industry. He was a logger in his teens, but he plowed every bit of his earnings into buying up land long before the area drew the attention of either conservationists or the US Department of the Interior.

According to an article she found, he'd decided to study the law in order to save on paying attorney's fees when negotiating contracts or fighting the growing conservation movement.

Her jaw dropped as she uncovered old Tyrone's involvement in one mind-bogglingly lucrative venture after another. He invested in Oklahoma oil wells, Texas cattle ranching, an investment firm based in Little Rock, and ended up being the personal attorney for a child-hood pal who had a hankering to expand his local five-and-dime into a nationwide discount chain.

But, unlike his humble friend, Powers had no qualms about trampling anyone who got in the way of his ambitions.

Still stewing on all she'd read, and fueled with a healthy dose of righteous indignation, Grace prepared for her foray into the PP&W offices with steely-eyed determination.

Tyrone had made certain his sons had become attorneys as well, and he'd established Powers, Powers & Walton with his famous client's favorite cousin's kid.

His sons went on to help him amass even more power and prestige. He invested heavily in land development all along what would later become the industrial corridor of northwest Arkansas. After encountering a stubborn homesteader who refused to sell his acreage, Tyrone went through various legal and political back channels to essentially swindle the poor fellow out of the land.

A fact that made her even more keyed up to go toe to toe with them. Or rather, cop to lawyer.

Smoothing her hair flat against her scalp, she coiled the ends into a no-nonsense bun at her nape and thought about how Trey Powers's grandfather had funded the campaigns of local politicians and eventually gotten his son William elected to state office and later the Senate.

She stepped into the pants that went with the suit her sister referred to as her "extra-basic cop suit" and pulled a plain white blouse with a button-down collar from its hanger. Her sister despaired of this look, but Faith had no idea how basic Grace was willing to be in order to convey the right message. Silks and high-heeled boots were for TV detectives.

The people at PP&W needed to understand she was the real deal.

Grace weighed her options as she surveyed her bag. She'd had the pants altered to make the belt loops large enough to accommodate an equipment belt if needed, but today it would be overkill. The boxy jacket hung loose enough to conceal the holster she wore at the small of her back when walking into a possibly tense situation, but if the meeting was seated, wearing a back holster would not only be extremely uncomfortable, but it would also make accessing her sidearm awkward.

The chances of needing her weapon in a roomful of attorneys were slim, but still, she wanted it on her body. Like the leather case holding her badge and credentials, it was part of the package. A person couldn't convincingly pull off full-on cop intimidation without carrying a sidearm.

So she opted for her ankle holster.

With the straps secured to her calf, she gave her socks one last tug. After the previous day's walk through the muck, she'd rinsed off her lug-soled oxfords and shined them up with one of the hotel washcloths. Glancing down at the scuffed toes, she gave a mental shrug. She'd done the best she could.

She reexamined her tote to be sure her cuffs, zip ties, notepad and tablet were in place, then pulled it from the seat of the sofa. Satisfied she had everything she needed, she checked her weapon, bent to insert it into the holster and secured it.

"Ready or not, here I come," she murmured as she walked out the hotel room door.

THE LARGE RECEPTION desk at Powers, Powers & Walton had the sort of sleek midcentury-modern design that looked both quintessential and cutting-edge. A young woman wearing a headset sat in the center of the command module answering phones and passing along messages with well-modulated, studiedly unruffled efficiency.

Grace waited until she finished putting a call through. She walked to the desk with her wallet open, flashing her badge and credentials. "Special Agent Grace Reed of the Arkansas State Police Criminal Investigation Division," she announced. "I'm here to see Trey Powers."

To her credit, the young woman didn't look at all fazed by either Grace's presence or pronouncement. Instead, she simply smiled and said, "One moment, please," in the same tone she used with the callers she dispatched with such alacrity.

She pressed a single fingertip to the earpiece of her headset. "Mrs. Branson? Special Agent Reed is here to see Mr. Powers." There was a pause, then the receptionist nodded. "Yes, ma'am. Right away."

Rising as smoothly as she spoke, she smiled at Grace. "If you'll follow me, Special Agent."

Grace pocketed her credentials and followed the young woman past a glass half wall separating the reception area from an open-plan office space. She eyeballed the series of doors that blocked off private offices at the other end of the space, assuming they'd head that way. Instead, the receptionist drew to a stop beside a set of oversize double doors.

"If you'll wait in here, please, Special Agent Reed,"

she said with a sweet smile. "Can I offer you coffee or tea?"

Grace spied a backlit mini fridge built into the coffee bar setup in the conference room, and a pitcher of water and an arrangement of glasses sat on the table. "No, thank you. Water is fine for me."

"Please help yourself."

The young woman disappeared, closing the door after her with a click. Grace gave a soft snort and strolled over to the large oval table dominating the room. A self-deprecating smile tugged at her lips. "So much for fear and intimidation."

She was about to pour a glass of water when the conference room door opened again.

"Special Agent Reed?" a man in his midfifties asked as he strode through the door. He was followed by another man who appeared to be ten years younger, six inches shorter and markedly rounder.

"I'm Harold Dennis, personal counsel to the Powers family," the older man announced. "This is my associate, Michelle Fraser."

Grace glanced back at the door as a woman closed it behind them. "Will Mr. Powers be joining us?"

Mr. Dennis shook his head. "I'm afraid Mr. Powers is in court this morning. His assistant asked we take the meeting with you. How can we be of help?"

He gestured for her to take a seat in one of the tall leather chairs. Grace set her bag down on the table with a heavy thud. "Were either of you in attendance at the crawfish boil Mr. Powers hosted last Friday evening?"

Ms. Fraser shook her head and glanced over at Mr. Dennis, as though he wondered if he'd missed an invitation. He, too, wagged his head, then answered. "No, ma'am."

"I'm not sure how you plan to be of help to me, then." Grace picked up her bag and hoisted it onto her shoulder again. "Can you tell me when I might be able to speak to Mr. Powers in person?"

"I don't handle his scheduling," Mr. Dennis replied, lifting a mocking brow.

"Fine," Grace said briskly. "If you'll point me in the direction of his assistant, I will make an appointment."

"Special Agent Reed, if you have questions for Mr. Powers, I'd be happy to convey them to him," Mr. Dennis offered.

"I'd prefer not to use an intermediary," she replied evenly.

"Perhaps if you were to submit the questions you have for Mr. Powers to me in writing," the older man continued, "we could clarify the timeline of Friday evening's festivities and hopefully fill in any blanks."

Grace offered him a cool smile. "I'll wait to speak to Mr. Powers in person."

"Your prerogative." Dennis inclined his head in a gesture she assumed was supposed to convey deference but somehow felt condescending.

"Ms. Fraser will introduce you to Serena, Mr. Powers's assistant, to coordinate a meeting when we are all available."

"Does Mr. Powers have reason to worry about speaking with police without counsel present?"

The older man shrugged and gave what was meant to appear as a helpless smile. "I don't have the vaguest idea what Mr. Powers worries about."

Tiring of the cat-and-mouse game, Grace nodded and turned to the other attorney. "If you would make the introduction, I would appreciate it."

Fifteen minutes later, she breezed past the sleek reception desk and out the doors, her temper simmering. Matthew had been right. It wasn't going to be easy to get near Trey Powers. But if the guard dogs at PP&W thought she would be put off by the runaround, they were sadly mistaken.

Chapter Ten

Grace Reed knew how to make an entrance, that was for sure. The minute she walked into the prosecuting attorney's offices, the air felt charged. The low murmur of voices paused for a few noticeable ticks of the clock. For the first time since he'd opened the folder containing a motion he intended to file in one of his cases, Matthew's concentration broke.

He had only planned to come into the office for a few hours to line things out for Nate, but it was already past noon and he was still up to his elbows in work. Without conscious thought, he rose from his chair as she approached his open door. Her expression might have looked neutral to anyone who hadn't spent the past two days studying her, but he knew at a glance whatever she had to tell him wasn't good.

Wordlessly, he gestured to the guest chair across from his desk once she closed the door. "What have you heard?" he asked, suddenly grateful for his own chair as his knees grew wobbly.

"I had a call from the Benton County coroner. The initial indication of blunt-force trauma was correct. Mallory struck or was struck by something."

"Before or after?"

"Hard to tell the exact timing, because she did aspirate water, but the angle, size and shape of the injury don't line up with hitting her head on a log or something submerged in the water."

He fidgeted with the pen he'd left beside a pad of legal paper. "And the angle, size and shape were?"

"It appears to be something wide and flat. The injury was to the side of her skull, behind and above her ear." She gestured to the general vicinity on her own head. "Not generally consistent with someone hitting their head after they've fallen into a body of water."

"Someone hit her with something," he concluded.

She raised her hands in a staying motion. "It's early days."

He slumped into his chair. "When will they release her?"

"He said probably the end of next week."

Matthew nodded, his mind instantly shifting to funeral arrangements, because it was far preferable to thinking about his sister's murder.

"Have you been to her apartment yet?"

Grace's question jarred him from his thoughts. "What?"

"Have you gone to Eureka Springs to start sorting out Mallory's belongings?" she repeated, her diction careful.

He shook his head, gestured to his laptop and the pad filled with notes beside him. "No, I was going to call her roommate when I finished this and make sure it was okay to head over there, but I got…drawn in."

Grace pursed her lips. He knew that look well. Had

worked with the police for too long. He wasn't getting the whole story.

"What? What am I missing?" he demanded.

She uncrossed her legs and sat forward in the chair, her elbows braced on her knees. "I want to be sure I'm clear. You have not been to the apartment Mallory shared with Kelli Simon, correct?"

He raised an eyebrow. The woman would have made a fine prosecutor if she'd been inclined. "I have not," he stated, matching her concise delivery.

"Someone has," she said grimly as she pushed back in the chair again. "Ms. Simon called me when I was on my way here. She says she came home for lunch and discovered someone had been in her apartment."

"Burglary?"

She shook her head. "No electronics or items of value taken."

He frowned. "What makes her think someone was there?"

"The place had been tossed."

"Tossed?"

"Someone went through the apartment looking for something."

He blinked. "Looking for what?"

The thin line of her mouth told him the detective had her guesses but was reluctant to share them with him outright. He tried a different tactic.

"Okay, so far this morning you've been told my sister likely died by being struck in the head with something…" He broke off, waiting patiently for her to supply at least a tidbit of information.

"Something smooth and flat," she said at last.

Matthew swallowed the unexpected rush of emotion that rose when he tried to envision Mallory being struck. He drew a deep breath, then blew it out on a huff.

"Flat and smooth," he repeated. "I'm going to assume before her body went into the water."

"You can make that assumption, but we have no way of being certain."

"And you are also telling me her apartment has been...ransacked?"

"Correct."

"But what you aren't saying is you have your suspicions about what they might be looking for, and you don't want to share them."

Grace startled. "It's more I'm debating how best to use the information."

"Against me?" he asked, incredulous.

"No. Against the person I suspect did this to her." He was still forming his next question when she raised a hand to stall him. "And no, I have no proof. No way of knowing my suspect had anything to do with an assault that may or may not have taken place, and no grounds to point any fingers."

Their gazes met and held, both of them all too acutely aware of the impotence of the moment.

"To make matters even more frustrating, I went to the PP&W office this morning."

His jaw dropped, but he quickly reeled in his surprise. "You did?"

She nodded. "Figured I'd storm the castle."

"How did it go?" he asked.

"I'll give you a guess for free," she said dismissively. "He wasn't in."

Grace touched the end of her nose, pointed to him. "I did get to meet with a man named Harold Dennis, who is apparently the legal counsel to the Powers family, and another attorney named Fraser."

"Not surprising." He resisted the urge to remind her he'd told her so, but only because he knew she could hear the subtext.

"I suppose not, but it was worth a try."

"No way they were going to let that happen."

She opened her hands. "All I wanted was a simple sit-down with a man who by all accounts was with her the evening of her disappearance."

"There's no such thing as a 'simple sit-down,' and you couldn't have been shocked to meet with his attorneys," Matthew insisted, not fooled for a minute.

The corner of her mouth twitched. "Okay, maybe I wasn't, but I was hoping I'd at least get him in the room with them."

"You'll have to come at him with something more than a desire for an informal chat."

"Right, but a girl can hope"

He frowned as he considered the possible reasons for the nonmeeting. "Fraser? I don't remember seeing anyone with that name among the associates. Fraser what?"

She shook her head. "Michelle Fraser."

Realization sent him back in his chair. "Whoa," he said quietly. "They must be worried."

Grace startled. "What makes you say so?"

"Michelle Fraser is the only attorney on the PP&W staff who specializes in criminal defense." He gave his head a bewildered shake. "You say her name three times out there," he said, pointing to the office beyond his door, "and people run for the holy water."

Grace nodded as the information sank in. "Interesting."

"Isn't it?" He eyed her narrowly. "I wonder what has them scared enough to bring her in this early in the game."

She hesitated only a moment. Then, leaning forward, she admitted, "I've been holding back on something I was thinking might get some traction with him."

"What's that?" he asked, perturbed to discover she hadn't been forthcoming with him, even though he knew it was standard for police to hold some evidence close until they knew it was most useful. "What do you have?"

"Your sister might have been pregnant."

The air whooshed from him. He had to blink until she came fully back into focus again. "What?"

"Mallory may have believed herself to be pregnant. I'm waiting for confirmation from the coroner's office, but Ms. Simon found a positive at-home pregnancy test in the trash the weekend Mallory went missing," she explained. "When I went to her apartment, the box was there with only one positive test wand."

"Only one?" he asked, his head spinning with the import of this new information.

"It was a two-pack. Women often take multiple tests to be certain."

"Oh, God. Mal—"

"I'm sorry to put it bluntly, and I'm sorry not to have divulged this information sooner, but your reaction," she said, pointing to his face, "is the kind of visceral response I want to get from Mr. Powers."

"Pregnant," Matthew repeated.

"Yes. Possibly." She hesitated, her breath catching on the last. "I'm sorry. You have to be aware we hold some evidence back."

"Evidence?" Turning the word into a question gained him no ground, but he was struggling to wrap his mind around the bombshell she'd dropped. He needed a minute to fit all the pieces together.

She leaned in again, her eyes locking with his. "I need you to think as a prosecutor and not as a brother. Can you?"

"I haven't thought like a brother in years," he said hoarsely. "I suppose I can put it off for a few more minutes."

She inclined her head and looked him full in the face again. "I am not a lake person. I didn't grow up on water, but wouldn't the waves…the nature of water… I don't think she was killed on the shore."

She held up a hand to stave off any questions, but it was unnecessary. He couldn't have conjured a plausible query if his life depended on it.

"Pure speculation on my part," she admitted. "I haven't spoken to anybody about this yet, but it's my gut feeling."

"Based on?" he prompted.

"She wouldn't have ended up in a place so remote unless she was pushed there by currents. Would she?"

Matthew thought about it for a moment. "I'm no expert, either, but it seems logical. They weren't on a busy spot in the lake," he went on, allowing his train of thought to lead him down the path of probability. "It's actually the tail end. Most of the action takes place up in Missouri. Here in Arkansas, the more popular lakes are Beaver and Bull Shoals."

She nodded. "But there would still be enough movement on Table Rock to cause currents. I mean, it's a lake created by a dam. They have release water from locks, right? Plus, there's good old Mother Nature," she conceded. "I assume the wind and weather also play a part in moving the water around."

He smiled at her simple assumption. "Mother Nature would be insulted at being downgraded to a supporting role. Wind and weather are always the most dominant forces on any body of water."

She gave him a ghost of a smile. "My apologies to Mother Nature. I meant no insult."

"Your theory is Mallory was killed out in open water and her body washed ashore," he concluded.

"Unless you can see some reason for Mallory to have been in such an isolated spot without a vehicle?" she challenged.

He shook his head. "No, I'm with you."

"The vehicle is bothering me," she admitted. "I can't get into PP&W again until Monday, but—"

"You're going back Monday?"

She grinned primly. "I have an appointment."

"You are tenacious."

"You have no idea," she replied gravely. "I got an address, so I thought I'd drive out to the lake and see how close I can get to the Powerses' property without stepping over any lines."

He chuckled. "You think being in the vicinity won't cross a line?"

She smiled. "I'll stick to the public highways. I'm nothing more than a tourist who doesn't want to spend her afternoon staring at a brick wall."

"And taking a careful look around."

"Exactly."

"What do I do about the apartment?" he asked.

"I'll call the sheriff's office and see when they'll let you in. Listen, I know the coroner said he'd need most of next week, but you can go ahead and contact the funeral home and start making arrangements."

He chewed the inside of his cheek. Neither of those options sounded as appealing as spending an afternoon snooping around with Grace Reed. "Would you like some company on your drive?" he asked as she rose.

"I wouldn't mind," she answered honestly, "but I think it's more important for you to be here now taking care of the arrangements."

"If I don't want to?"

Her smile was tinged with sadness. "Understandable, but necessary. I'm going poking around, and poking around can get a person in trouble. I can take the heat, but it would be different for you."

He didn't want to get on the bad side of the Powers family.

"Hold tight for this afternoon. Let me see what I can sniff out on my own. I'll report back if there's anything of interest," she promised.

Matthew bobbed his head as he rose from his chair as well. "Maybe we can have dinner tonight when you get back." She looked at him with such surprise, he realized she'd been caught completely off guard by the invitation. "I mean, you can catch me up on anything you learn, and I can fill you in on where I'm at."

Her shoulders dropped, and Matthew felt a strong wave of disappointment as he braced for the rejection sure to come.

To his amazement, she nodded. "Okay, sounds good. Text me when and where."

"Will do."

She paused in the doorway, gripping the handle. "You want this open or closed when I go?"

Matthew stared at the door for a moment. He usually worked with it open, but he was feeling too raw to leave himself exposed to the prying eyes of his coworkers. "Closed would be great, thanks."

When she was gone, he stared at the blank panel of wood shutting out the rest of the world. In the silence, his mind started to whirl.

Mallory was dead.

Mallory might have been pregnant.

Mallory was most likely murdered.

And her big brother was going to help make sure the person who did it faced justice.

"So no big revelations," he concluded, reaching for a second slice of the Chicago-style pizza they'd ordered for dinner.

"No, couldn't even see the house from the road, but given what I saw on the map, I didn't truly expect to. I just wanted to get a feel for the area." Grace wiped her fingers on a paper napkin. "I can't believe you can eat two pieces of this."

He glanced down at his plate. "Some people can't eat when they're stressed. I can't stop," he confessed. "I'll probably only make it through half, but one wasn't enough."

"I get you." She smiled ruefully at the remaining pizza and sat back. "It was delicious. I've never had Chicago-style pizza."

"This area is full of transplants," he said, using the edge of his fork to cut off a hunk of pizza. "The owners used to work at one of the popular places in Chicago. When they decided to go into the restaurant business here, they stuck to their niche. People who used to live up north flock to it, and some of us natives have turned to the dark side."

"And the dark side is the side that puts the sauce on top?" she asked, sounding amused.

"Exactly."

"So, you were asking about how my day went. How about yours? Were you able to get arrangements sorted?"

Matthew set his fork down on the edge of his plate. "Yes." Their gazes met and held. "The coroner said he spoke to you. She was pregnant."

"Yes," Grace said softly. Then she added, "I'm sorry for your loss."

Her sincerity in delivering the trite expression nearly broke him. For most of the afternoon, he'd been able to think about nothing but the nieces and nephews he'd never imagined and now would never have. The sister he'd never truly understand. And the answers they might never get.

"Listen, Grace," he began, shifting forward on the springy seat of the booth.

"No good proposition ever starts with the word *listen*," she said dryly.

"It's not a proposition as much as a request," he amended.

"Go on."

"I'd like to come with you to PP&W Monday."

"I thought you wanted to avoid getting involved there?"

"As a prosecutor, it's not the wisest thing," he admitted, rubbing a hand over his mouth. "But in this case, I'm not the prosecutor. I'm her brother."

"You realize I don't usually bring members of a victim's family along on interviews, right?"

"I get that, but… I'm hip to all the lawyer tricks. I can tell you which questions they'll be trying to evade and how to translate the nonanswers—"

"And you don't think I have the same skill set?"

He could she was torn between being insulted and amused, so he rushed in for damage control.

"No, no. Not at all. I think…two sets of eyes and ears," he finished lamely.

"You feel like you need to do something."

"Yes." He stared down at the untouched slice of pizza on his plate and wondered how in the world he'd thought he could eat another bite.

Without asking, Grace caught the attention of their server and pantomimed their need for a to-go box.

"Tell you what. You go home and sleep on it, and I'll call you in the morning. If you still feel the same way, we'll discuss the possibility of playing good cop, bad lawyer with them."

"Sounds fair."

"I'm not entirely certain I'll get to meet with Powers. He might stonewall me again."

"Oh, he'll meet with you," Matthew said grimly. "His ego won't let him dodge twice."

Her eyebrows rose. "You think?"

Their server deftly boxed the remaining pizza—including his untouched slice—and slid the folder containing the check onto the table.

She reached for it, but he was faster.

"I have a per diem," she said stiffly.

"I coerced you into meeting the grieving brother for dinner. The least I can do is buy you a slice of pizza and half a glass of wine."

"Is that what this is?" she asked, pinning him with a stare.

"I—I probably didn't do as much for Mallory as I could have…when she was…" He trailed off.

"Most of us don't," she said quietly. He looked up, confused, and she gave him a rueful smile. "We don't tell the people we love how we feel about them often enough."

He winced. "I wasn't sure how I felt about Mallory, period. Our relationship was confusing and often frustrating."

"Family is family. We don't get to choose the one that fits best. We have to figure out how to make it work."

"I didn't do a good job of making things work."

She inclined her head. "It feels that way now, but maybe one day you'll cut yourself some slack. Relationships are two-sided." She took a sip of her mostly untouched wine, grabbed the pizza box and started to slide from the booth. "Come on. It's been a long day, and we both have a lot to think about."

He shoved a couple of bills into the folder and followed her lead. On the sidewalk outside the restaurant, she turned and shoved the box into his hands. "Go home. Don't drink any more alcohol, but maybe eat at least one more slice of pizza if you feel up to it. Sleep as well as you can. We'll talk in the morning."

Her concise delivery should have thrown him off, but it felt oddly good to be given a list of simple instructions to follow.

"Will do."

"Good night, Counselor."

To his surprise, she gave his arm a gentle squeeze of consolation as she moved past him in the direction of her car. He turned and watched as the lights flashed. She climbed into the driver's seat. A minute later, she pulled away without so much as another glance in his direction.

He stood there and waited until her taillights blended in with traffic. Heaving a sigh, he headed for his own car. He'd been given his orders, and Matthew figured it couldn't hurt to follow them.

Chapter Eleven

When Grace walked into the conference room at PP&W again, she wasn't the least bit impressed by her surroundings. This made her feel slightly more in control. Plus, she wasn't alone. Matthew stood at her side, tall and somber in a gray suit and striped tie.

Neither of them was surprised to be met with a phalanx of attorneys when they were ushered into the room. She was scanning to see if their hotshot criminal defense attorney was among them when a man who could only be Trey Powers stepped away from the crowd. He looked exactly as she imagined him—young, handsome, tanned from his days on the lake, confident from the day he was born. He had brown hair with gold tips that looked like they hadn't been created by Mother Nature and blue eyes so light they were almost silver.

"Mr. Powers," she said, taking his proffered hand. "Thank you for meeting with me today."

"I'm sorry I wasn't in yesterday. When His Honor calls, we run."

He glanced past her shoulder, and the confusion that clouded his expression told her he'd spotted Matthew. He quickly wiped the slate clean. "I'm Trey Powers," he said, extending his hand like an eager car salesman. "It feels like we've met before somewhere," he continued with a vague shake of his head.

"Mr. Murray is Mallory Murray's brother," Grace informed him.

The information seemed to bring Powers up short. He froze for a moment, his hand still clasping Matthew's. "Brother?"

To his credit, Matthew didn't flinch. Nor did he respond to the puzzled inquiry. Grace was relieved he was sticking to his promise to let her do the talking. "Yes, Ms. Murray was Mr. Murray's younger sister."

"Was?" Powers divided a glance between her and Matthew, his expression one of unconvincing concern. Grace could only assume he'd been tipped off by the county coroner. Not a shocker. If the family was as tied in as Matthew said they were, they would have been tipped off about the recovery as soon as she requested the transfer to Benton County. Maybe sooner.

Trey glanced back at one of the immaculately clad attorneys who'd moved in behind him. Grace nodded a greeting to Harold Dennis, then gestured to the table. "If we could take a seat?"

"Of course," Mr. Dennis replied, speaking for the entire group.

At her direction, they quickly scattered to seats around the table, the PP&W attorneys flanking Trey and taking up almost all the seats on one side of the table.

Mr. Dennis rattled off a flurry of introductions, most of which were a jumble she'd have to sort out later, but she made sure to meet Ms. Fraser's eyes squarely. She wanted the criminal defense expert to know she'd been pointed out. The other woman stared back at her with cool blue eyes, her face impassive.

She also spotted Taylor Greene, the young brunette Steve had identified from the headshots they'd showed him on their trip back to Stubby's, but she didn't see the young man with glasses he'd said was with them.

Matthew nodded to her as they took chairs at the center of the opposite side, facing them. The side eye he'd given Taylor told her he'd recognized Ms. Greene, too.

Grace took a moment to pull her notepad out of her tote and flip it open to her notes. She had her tablet, but since the others had chosen to go analog with pens and pads of paper arrayed in front of them, Grace was more than happy to let them set the tenor of the meeting. She was on a fishing expedition here. No sense in putting them on the defensive from the get-go.

"I'm afraid Ms. Murray's body was found early Friday morning," Grace announced, her eyes fixed on Trey Powers.

The attorneys murmured and muttered a mixture of surprise and condolences, but Grace kept her gaze locked on target.

"Her body?" Trey fell back in his chair and scraped a hand over his face, seeming to process the implication.

"Yes, sir," she responded, sliding a glance to the young woman at the end of the table.

Ms. Greene stared down at the legal pad and pen squared away in front of her, her face pale and her lips pressed into a thin line. Steve had been right to card her. Despite the severe black suit she wore, she looked considerably younger than the men around her.

Grace dragged her attention away from Taylor Greene and back to Powers. "Ms. Murray is dead."

Trey leaned in, concern knitting his brow as he laced his fingers together and propped them on the glossy table. "I'm sorry to hear. Mallory was a wonderful girl," he said, pointing the last comment directly to Matthew.

"Thank you," Matthew replied quietly.

"We understand Ms. Murray attended a party at your family's home on Table Rock Lake last Friday evening," she continued.

Trey didn't bother with any evasion. "Yes. We ran into her at Stubby's when we were on our way out there, and she was game to come along."

"Stubby's Bar and Grill on Highway 62?"

"Yes, ma'am," Powers replied.

Grace made a show of checking her notebook. "And she was working a shift at Stubby's that night?"

Trey's mouth twitched, but a sharp glance from Mr. Dennis had him smoothing his expression out again. "Yes. As I told you when we spoke on the phone, I invited her to join us."

"But she didn't ride with you or any of your other guests?"

"No, I don't believe so," he replied evenly. "Mallory liked to come and go as she pleased."

He turned to look at Mr. Dennis, but Grace saw his gaze slide to one of the other young lawyers. This one looked something like Powers's budget doppelgänger. He wore a suit in the same shade of bright blue. His hair was cut in a similar style but was noticeably thinner than Trey's. She couldn't quite ID the guy from the photos on the website.

She wouldn't get any further with this line of questioning until Mallory's vehicle was found, so Grace switched tactics.

"How long have you and Ms. Murray been acquainted?"

Powers blinked. The changeup worked. "Uh…" His focus again shifted to Mr. Dennis. When the attorney nodded his approval, Trey opened his hands and looked up at the ceiling, searching his memory. "Um, years. I think when we first met, she was still in high school." He paused for a second, then shook his head. "Or recently graduated."

Beside her, Matthew tensed.

"And how did you meet?" Grace asked.

"She was a waitress at Stubby's Bar and Grill. Has been forever," he said dismissively.

"And you frequented the establishment?"

He shrugged. "Everyone does."

Satisfied she had established the tenure of their acquaintance, she decided not to push on the more personal aspects. The last thing Grace wanted was for Trey Powers to twig to the notion she knew about a possible pregnancy.

"Mr. Powers, does your family keep a boat at your lake house?" she asked.

She saw Mr. Dennis stiffen, but before the older man could counsel his client, Trey chuckled and volunteered an answer. "We have four."

Grace did her best not to appear impressed by the number he tossed out with such brazen confidence, but it was hard not to be. Four boats seemed excessive for a lake in the middle of the Ozarks. "Four?"

Mr. Dennis tapped his pen on the legal pad in front of him, but Powers blustered on, his ego clearly in the driver's seat. "Yes, we have a pontoon boat, a johnboat, my father's bass boat and my boat."

Grace noted he didn't volunteer what type of boat his was precisely. "Your boat? What kind of boat do you have?"

"A ski boat," he said, tossing it off with a one-shouldered shrug.

His studied nonchalance told her it was most likely the top of the line as far as ski boats were concerned, but she could care less. She only wanted to confirm whether watercraft were available to take the partygoers out onto the lake the previous Friday night. "And were any of the boats in use during the party?"

"Almost all of them at one point or another," Trey responded, glancing at his friends with a chuckle. "We're all water rats."

"Well, not all of us," the young man beside Trey drawled with a snigger.

"Right." Trey let out a short laugh. "All except for Josh. He's not much of a boat guy. Can barely handle the jon-boat."

She made a note. She knew from growing up in a state where hunting was practically a religion that a joh-boat was a flat-bottomed boat equipped with an outboard motor. People used them for duck hunting or fishing along shorelines. "Josh?" she asked, glancing from one man to another.

"What do you expect from a guy from Missouri?" Powers's doppelgänger chimed in.

A couple of the other attorneys chuckled, but Grace's

curiosity was piqued. The comment was clearly meant as an insult.

"Josh?" she asked, glancing from one man to another.

"Joshua Potter," Harold Dennis supplied. "Another one of our associates."

"Is he not here?"

"He's out of town on behalf of a client," Mr. Dennis explained.

"I see." Grace made a note, then turned to the attorney beside Trey Powers. "I'm sorry, I don't believe I caught your name."

The young man straightened in his seat. He clearly didn't appreciate being overlooked. "Chet Barrow. I'm an associate here at the firm."

"And you attended the crawfish boil?" she persisted.

"Yes, ma'am."

"And this Josh, did he have an accident with the boat?" she asked, eyebrows raised.

"No, not an accident," Trey answered, drawing all eyes back to him. "He took a girl out as the sun was setting and got the prop tangled up in the weeds. They needed to be towed away from shore."

The image of the muddy, grass-flattened bank where Mallory's body had been found sprang to mind.

"Near the house, or somewhere else on the lake?" she asked.

At this juncture, Mr. Dennis interceded. "I fail to see the relevance of this line of questioning, Agent Reed."

"Oh, I'm sorry," Grace said, insincerity dripping from every word. "Did I not make myself clear earlier? Mallory Murray's body was discovered by a fisherman. It had been washed ashore in one of the inlets on Table Rock Lake."

Before any of the younger attorneys could respond, Mr. Dennis jumped in to set the course of the conversation. "I'm terribly sorry to hear, but Agent Reed, I don't see how this young lady's unfortunate death can be tied directly to my client."

Grace gave her head a shake and opened her hands palm up. "I didn't mean to imply I was connecting your client directly to Ms. Murray's death. I was simply establishing where she might have spent her last hours and how she might have gotten out onto the lake."

"Do we have evidence she was out on the lake?" Mr. Dennis challenged. "Perhaps she fell into the water from the shore."

"I don't," Grace admitted, hoping by throwing this bone, they might be more inclined to be forthcoming about the events of the night.

"Was Ms. Murray's body found on or near the property owned by the Powers family?" Mr. Dennis pressed.

Grace shook her head again. "She was found on an inlet is located a few miles to the east of the Powerses' property."

"So you could say this entire meeting is a fishing expedition of sorts," Mr. Dennis said stiffly. He closed his leather portfolio and rose from his chair. The other attorneys scrambled to follow his lead.

Turning his attention to Matthew, Harold Dennis inclined his head a fraction of an inch. "I'm sure I speak for all of us when I say I'm terribly sorry to hear about your sister's death, Mr. Murray. I understand your desire to get answers as to what might have happened to her, but I don't believe you'll find them here."

Having spoken his piece, he focused on Grace.

"If you'll excuse us, Agent Reed," he said firmly. "I believe that's all the time we have today."

The entire Powers team collected their portfolios and murmured goodbyes.

"I wish you luck with your investigation," Mr. Dennis continued. "If you have any further questions for my client, I would appreciate it if you would direct them to me as his counsel."

Grace didn't bristle. She didn't try to play the heavy. There was no point at this juncture. She had nothing but conjecture and a secret in her back pocket. If she made this interaction into a confrontation, she'd only be closing off the possibility of further conversation.

She rose and extended her hand first to Trey Powers, then to his attorney, making direct eye contact with each of them. "Of course. I appreciate your help. And if you or any of your friends think of anything you think might be helpful, I would appreciate a call."

With that, she pulled a handful of business cards from her suit pocket and offered one to each attorney as they passed, making sure to press one into Taylor Greene's palm. The young woman hurried from the room, her head bowed.

Beside her, Matthew sat still as a statue. Grace reclaimed the seat next to him, her eyes fixed on the back of Trey Powers's head as he leaned in and whispered something to the attorney who was clearly emulating the heir apparent in style. Their throaty chuckles carried back into the room before the heavy wooden door closed behind them.

Matthew turned on her, his eyes alight with righteous indignation. "You had him in a room and that's all you're going to ask? Of course they have boats. It's a lake house."

"Yes, but I wasn't sure how many or what kind," Grace said, unruffled by his ire. "Now I have specifics for a search warrant." She stared into his angry eyes, careful to keep her own expression calm and steady. She'd been confronted by too many frustrated and un- happy family members to take his displeasure person- ally. "Trust me, I have plenty to start with."

"If you think you're going to get a search warrant for their estate or any of those boats from a local judge, you're cracked," he said as she gathered her things.

She lowered her voice. "I'm not cracked. But this is not the place to discuss this."

She picked up her tote bag and rose from the chair again. Looking down at him, she heaved a heavy sigh. "I'm not sure what you expected to happen in this meet- ing, but I can tell you it went exactly as I anticipated. You're going to have to trust me. I am good at my job. And in case you've forgotten what that is, my job is to collect enough solid, irrefutable evidence for people like you to do *your* job."

Matthew blew out a breath, his shoulders sagging as he visibly deflated. "I'm sorry," he murmured.

Grace nudged his chair. "Come on. We can talk more in the car."

He pushed back his chair and followed her from the room.

Once they were seated in her state-issued SUV, he looked over at her. "What's your plan? Aside from the fact the circuit court judge for this area is the Walton in Powers, Powers & Walton, I promise you there isn't a judge in a five-county area whose robes weren't financed by the Powers family."

"I'll find a judge who isn't tied to the Powers purse strings," she said evenly. He scoffed, and she shook her head. "You forget, I'm not confined to county lines. This is a state investigation, and surely somewhere in the state of Arkansas I should be able to find one judge they don't own."

"Good luck," he said disparagingly.

"As a matter of fact, I already have a couple in mind." She started the car and put it into gear. "And I bet if you stop letting them get into your head, you can probably come up with other possibilities."

"They aren't in my head," he shot back, defensive.

"They are. You're as awed by them as Mallory was, but in a different way," she said, sliding him a glance as she pulled from the parking lot. "Don't let the flash and bluster blind you. That guy in there is scared. Scared enough to assemble his own dream team to take a simple meeting with a lowly detective from the state police."

"I doubt he goes anywhere without an entourage," Matthew responded dully.

Grace spared him another glance but found rather than sulking, he appeared thoughtful. She smiled. She could almost see the gears turning in his head.

"Right," she said encouragingly. "And when there's a crowd, there's bound to be a witness. It's only a matter of watching and waiting."

He inspected her as she pulled out onto the street. "You already have a mark," he concluded.

She nodded. "Yep."

"The one at the end…the woman Steve ID'd," he said slowly.

Grace nodded as he slotted the puzzle pieces into place. "Taylor Greene. The one he carded when they came into Stubby's."

She could feel his gaze on her, warm and appraising. "You think she'll roll?"

"I think she's the weakest link."

"What makes you say so?" he asked, sounding genuinely curious.

Grace smiled. "Because she's either hopelessly in love with Trey Powers or she loathes him," she answered. "I only have to figure out which buttons to push." She let her statement hang there for a moment, then she glanced over at him as she switched tacks. "Do me a favor?"

"Sure, what can I do?"

"Petition your friend Judge Walton for those search warrants?"

He scoffed. "Why? I told you he'll never issue them."

"I want the Powers team to think they have me stymied. The cockier they get, the more likely they are to slip up."

"I'm not sure," he began.

She understood his hesitance but wasn't about to let him off the hook. If they were going to unravel the sequence of events surrounding Mallory's death, they would have to start picking at the knot. If she went to another judge without trying to act locally, it might arouse suspicion with the Powers team. If they were thwarted by the local judge and went elsewhere to get the warrants, it was possible the folks at PP&W would consider them little more than an annoyance.

"It could prove to be tricky for me," Matthew said quietly.

"I understand. I'll ask someone in my office to file the paperwork," she offered, turning to watch his reaction as she stopped at a light.

His rejection was almost instantaneous. "I need to do something…"

"You are even if you aren't pushing the paperwork," she assured him. "Think of it this way—if getting to Trey Powers is the goal, I'm going to need to get around his defenders. I need you to be my point man. Set a pick or two, to speak."

He looked over at her in surprise. "You speak basketball?"

She chortled and pressed the accelerator. "I hit five-ten in the sixth grade. What do you think?"

"I think I'm even more impressed than I was before," he said, sounding truly admiring.

Grace smiled but kept her eyes on the road. "Yeah, well, wait until you see me dunk."

Chapter Twelve

"Good morning."

Matthew looked up to find his boss hovering in his doorway. "Morning."

"I thought you were taking some days off," Nate commented, confusion puckering his forehead. He stepped inside and closed the door behind him.

"I'm still waiting for the coroner to release Mallory's body," he explained, instinctively hitting the save icon and lowering the screen of his laptop until it was mostly closed. He'd been reviewing the timeline they'd pieced together from Friday night through the meeting at PP&W, and he didn't want Nate to know he'd been anywhere near the firm if he didn't have to. "I'm going to Eureka Springs this evening to gather Mallory's things."

"Ah, I see," Nate replied quietly. "I still can't believe I didn't know you had a sister."

Matthew eyed him curiously. They'd always been friendly, but they weren't exactly friends. "I don't know if *you* have siblings," he pointed out. "I mean, I know you're married and have kids. I guess people tend to talk about more about their kids at work."

Nate raised both eyebrows. "I suppose." Jerking his chin up, his gaze fixed on Matthew's laptop. "Are you working on anything we can help you with? I can reassign cases if you need me to."

Matthew shook his head. "Nah. Catching up on some paperwork while I play the waiting game."

His boss gave another slow nod. "I hear you and the investigating officer looking into your sister's death visited PP&W."

Matthew didn't flinch. Years of working with Nate had prepared him for this roundabout conversation.

"Yeah, we did." He offered no more explanation. If Nate wanted to know something specific, he'd have to ask an actual question.

"Unusual," the prosecuting attorney said, propping his shoulder against the door frame in a studiously casual pose. Matthew felt an urge to jump up and push him off balance.

"Is it?" he returned evenly.

Nate snorted. They were both aware the police didn't take grieving family members along on witness interviews. "Be careful, Matt."

Matthew stiffened, both at the warning and the nickname he never used. Nate knew he hated it.

"Be careful? I never opened my mouth."

It was close enough to the truth. He hadn't asked any of the questions or done more than murmur thanks for the condolences offered by people in the room.

"You know what I mean," Nate said, pushing away from the door frame and drawing himself up to his full height. "You have plans for the future. Because of those plans, you've purposefully avoided going head to head with PP&W. Don't turn yourself into an adversary now."

"I didn't realize my presence would be seen as adversarial," Matthew replied disingenuously.

Nate's usually smiling mouth thinned into a line. "You're acting foolish and reckless," he observed. "I never pegged you for either of those things."

Matthew was saved from answering by the blare of his phone. The sound sliced through the tension in the room and bounced off the walls, disarmingly jubilant against the backdrop of the conversation.

Normally he would have silenced it without a glance when talking with Nate, but he seized it as a ticket out of their conversation. A peek at the screen showed the caller to be Grace. He accepted the call but said only, "Hey, can you give me a moment?"

"Sure," she replied.

Muting the phone, Matthew looked back at the man hovering in his doorway. "Don't worry. I have no intention of being foolish or reckless," he stated, holding Nate's gaze.

The other man nodded once and took a step back. "Good. I'll let you get to your call." He rapped two knuckles against the door frame. "Take it easy on yourself. We'll all be here, and all of this will be waiting for you." He opened the office door, then gestured grandiosely to the open-plan office humming with activity.

"Yeah." Matthew nodded and forced himself to return the smile. "The bad guys never take a day off."

"Truth," Nate called over his shoulder as he walked away.

Matthew waited until he was certain the other man was gone, then he unmuted the call. "Grace?"

"Yes, is this a bad time?"

"No, I had to finish a conversation."

He rocked back in his chair and peered out his open office door to be sure no one was lurking nearby. "You know what? I think I'm going to get out of here."

"Oh?"

He lowered his voice as he sandwiched the phone between his ear and shoulder. "Somehow, Nate knew I was at PP&W this morning. He also made it clear he didn't approve of my being there."

"Does it matter if he approves or not?" Grace asked.

"To a certain extent. The man is my boss."

"You shouldn't be in the office anyway."

"It's here or an empty apartment," he said grimly. "I thought it might be better to be around people, but now I don't know."

"How about one person?" she asked.

"Excuse me?"

"How about being around one person?" She paused, and Matthew found himself holding his breath until she spoke again. "I'm at the StayOn extended stay over on Washington Street. I've got a whole office set up here, complete with a whiteboard and markers."

"You're inviting me to come there to work?"

"I'm inviting you to come here and work on your sister's case," she said, spelling it out for him. "I'm afraid I have some not-great news."

"Well, that seems to be the theme this week."

"I know."

"Might as well hit me with it."

"Maybe your paranoia is rubbing off on me, but I don't want to get into details over the phone," she said, overenunciating the last few words to make her point. "Can you meet me here?"

Instantly on guard, he demanded, "Give me a rough idea."

"They found Mallory's car."

Something about her lack of inflection set his antennae twitching. "And?"

"It was in a lake."

"Wow. I wish I could say I was shocked," Matthew said stiffly.

"Yeah. Unfortunately, it's not going to make our quest to get access to the Powers property any easier," she said in a voice tinged with genuine regret.

"No? Why not?" he asked, closing the lid of his laptop and reaching for his messenger bag in one practiced movement. He had the computer jammed halfway in the pouch when she finally broke the news.

"Wrong lake."

"WHERE WAS IT?" he pressed when she opened the door to room 152.

"Hello to you, too." She stepped back and waved him into the room. The minute the door slammed shut behind him, she pointed to a whiteboard propped on the sofa. "Beaver Lake. Not far off Highway 62."

"Beaver Lake?" he repeated, unable to process the incongruity.

"Yeah. On the west side. I'm guessing about fifteen miles from the Powers place as the crow flies, but it would take longer to get there on the highway."

He dropped his bag at the base of the breakfast bar. Moving into the suite's living area, he propped his hands on his hips. "No more than five minutes from

Stubby's," he murmured. "We've been driving back and forth past it all week."

"We wouldn't have seen anything. We didn't go down to Beaver Lake," she reminded him. "A guy training to re-up his scuba certification caught sight of the license plate and noticed the tag was current."

Matthew dropped down onto one of the barely padded stools and gazed at her. "She paid her registration. For once, Mallory didn't flake on something."

He scrubbed his face. A morass of incredulity and self-recrimination for continuing to think poorly of his sister, even in death, threatened to smother him.

Grace blew out a breath. "I know you said you'd do it, but I asked one of my colleagues to request the search warrants for the Powerses' house and boats from Judge Walton this morning," she informed him. "Thankfully, this information had not yet come to light. Maybe there's a chance."

"A snowball's chance," Matthew said grudgingly. "Where is the car now?"

"It's being hauled to impound on a flatbed. We had a forensic diver go in and recover anything they could find in the glove box and console. They'll also work on the car to see if they can recover any prints, hair, other DNA."

Matthew felt a flicker of hope sputter to life in his chest. "Depending on how well contained the cabin was, they may be able to get some fingerprint residue," he said, giving voice to the flutter of optimism.

"The windows were rolled down," she informed him, her expression somber. "The team tells me there are some other things they can do, but I'm betting we won't find any evidence of anyone other than Mallory in her car. Plus, I doubt Trey Powers was the kind to go riding around town in his gal pal's subcompact."

"Definitely not," he agreed. "The guy drives a Porsche."

"The team tells me whoever sank this car knew what they were doing."

"Professionals?" He was tempted to scoff at the idea but was unable to rule out the possibility of Powers hiring someone to ditch the vehicle.

"I can't say professionals, but we can be pretty sure Mallory didn't roll all her windows down, drive into Beaver Lake, swim to shore, hitch a ride over to Table Rock and bash herself in the back of the head with something smooth and flat until she fell into the water," she said, brusque with impatience.

"Right. It doesn't make sense."

"I'm figuring they didn't want that car found anywhere near the Powers place. Either way, something stinks like old fish. I've called in a favor with some IT people I know. They may be able to go deeper with Mallory's social media and try to dig some things out."

"Cool."

"Let's compare notes and impressions. We can order some food and wait for either forensics or the judge to give us something more to go on. Have you eaten today?"

Matthew's stomach flipped at the mention of food. He couldn't focus on food. Bigger questions preyed on his mind.

"And if forensics comes up empty?" he couldn't resist asking. "What if there's no evidence pointing to Trey Powers?"

"We'll get something."

"Even with the pregnancy, I'm not sure we can prove the child was his," he argued.

"You don't seem to have much faith in science," she said tartly.

"I believe in science, but we don't know how pregnant she was. My gut tells me we're not going to get lucky enough to connect one shred of Trey Powers's DNA to my sister."

"You give him far more credit than he's due, Matthew. This guy is only human. His friends and colleagues are, too. They aren't supervillains from a comic book. They're people. And if there's one fact we know for certain about people, it's that somewhere along the line, they all screw up."

Matthew swallowed hard, slid off the stool and stalked over to the whiteboard she had propped on what appeared to be a rock-hard sofa. Looking at the dry-erase board covered in messy scrawl and squiggling lines connecting one fact to another was oddly calming. Forcing himself to inhale and exhale, he nodded.

"Yeah, they do."

She stepped up beside him, her shoulder grazing his as they both stared at the board. "How many impossible cases have you seen break open because one thing got overlooked?"

"Too many."

"And how many have you seen break wide-open because somebody refused to blink when it came down to playing chicken? There's no hiding the truth entirely.

Somebody knows what happened to Mallory, and they are nothing more or less than a human being."

He gave her a half smile to go with his sidelong glance. "You make a good case, Agent Reed. Are you sure you didn't miss your calling? The ability to spin a logic-defying situation makes a good lawyer."

She leaned forward to adjust the positioning of a magnet she'd used to tack down the edge of an Arkansas highway map. "The problem is, I have a moral compass." She spoke over her shoulder at him, smirking.

"Yeah, they can be pesky," he agreed with a shrug.

"I think I need a sandwich." She pulled her phone from her pocket and wandered back to the kitchenette. "Sandwiches work for you?"

To his surprise, his stomach answered with a gurgle. Pursing his lips, he stared at the map, his gaze tracking the distance between the western shore of Beaver Lake and the trailing inlets of Table Rock. The end of the lake stretched across state lines from Missouri like grasping fingers.

"Works for me," he agreed distractedly. "You know, it doesn't take long to get from one lake to the other if you know the back roads."

"Oh, yeah?" Her brows lifted as she looked up from her phone. "Maybe we start by looking at any of Trey's buddies who grew up around here." She returned her attention to the screen. "I'm ordering Italian subs."

"Perfect." Turning on his heel, Matthew moved back to the bar, where he pulled his laptop from his bag and opened it. "I'm pretty sure the guy who was in there this morning—whatever his name was Barrow?—I think

I read on the website he's an East Coaster. Probably a prep school pal or something."

She snorted softly but continued to process their order. "Funny, I always imagined those guys as being ultraconfident, but he came across as…"

"Needy?" Matthew asked as he clicked through to the PP&W staff photos.

"I was thinking sad, but needy works, too," she murmured. "Definitely a hanger-on." Her phone chimed, and she looked up with a smile. "There. Sustenance is on the way."

She moved back to her board. "Okay, now we have Taylor Greene at the bar, the party and in the meeting. What's her story?"

Matthew clicked over to the photo of the wholesome-looking brunette. "Looks like the girl-next-door type."

"For some reason, I'm always more suspicious of the girl-next-door types," Grace murmured as she squinted at the board.

He chuckled. "Why am I not surprised?"

She looked over her shoulder at him. "You think you have me pegged, Counselor?"

For a moment he was dumbstruck again by how attractive he found her. Confidence and competence—they were as much a part of her as her strikingly dark brown eyes or the smattering of freckles across her nose. And the whole package was a potent one.

"Not at all. I'm simply assuming you're suspicious by nature. Occupational hazard."

She seemed to give thought consideration. "Yeah, okay. I can admit I am." She moved a note she'd made about the car and photo of Mallory printed from her

PicturSpam account aside, then picked up one of the markers scattered on the coffee table.

"The Powers place is here." She pointed to the spot marked with a red dot on the map. "Her body was found here," she said, jabbing a finger at a second dot to the north and east of the spit of land where the first Tyrone Powers had built his family fortress. She trailed the same fingertip along Highway 62, past the junction where Highway 37 took people up into Missouri and back down toward the town of Garfield. "You and Mallory grew up around here?" She tapped the map.

"Yes, but not in town. Out off the highway on the Beaver Lake side," he clarified.

"Her car was found here."

She marked the spot on the western shore with a black X. "Would have been closer to dump it on the east side."

"Definitely more accessible." Matthew squinted at the spot she'd marked. "There's more development on the dam side. Campgrounds, resorts—"

"But there would also be people who might notice someone pushing a car off into the water," she concluded.

"Been a while since I've been over there, but the car was found on the west side. North end." He tapped his lips with his forefinger. "There used to be only one road in up there. May still be if it's still timber company land." He peered at the map. "You're right. We need to take a closer look at anyone connected to Trey or PP&W who grew up in the area."

"Or at least vacationed here regularly."

"Right." Matthew went back to the bar to reclaim his

laptop. "Lake people, at least the regulars, would know the area as well as the locals."

"Now we have something to dig into while we wait for our food," she said, picking up the board and moving it to lean against the wall. "Have a seat. I'll grab my notes and a couple bottles of water."

Matthew watched her move about the room, collecting everything she might need in order to keep up her pursuit. She'd been correct to coerce him into coming here to work. This was neutral territory, safe from the office and local politics. And two heads were far better than one. Particularly when his hadn't been entirely in the game. Until now.

He'd been laboring under the delusion he could play both sides—save his sister and avoid crossing swords with the Powers family for the sake of his career ambitions. But it was never going to be possible.

Grace and her unerring moral compass were pointing him toward a different future than he'd envisioned, and he wasn't certain he was grateful for it. But he was grateful Mallory had Grace to stand up for her.

"Hey, Grace?"

"Hmm?" she said as she pulled a tablet and a power cord from her bag.

"Thanks for this," he said, his voice catching on the last. He cleared his throat. "For everything, but mostly for getting me out of the office and over here. I didn't realize how much I needed a change of scenery."

She smiled, and her dark eyes lit with amusement. "If this is a change of scenery for you, you need to get out more, Mr. Murray."

Her phone rang, and she pulled it from her pocket.

She shot him a glance and made a face when she saw who was calling. "Let's see if we got our warrants, shall we?" She accepted the call and tapped for the icon to send it to speaker. "Any luck, Jim?"

"It's a no-go with Judge Walton, Grace," a man said without preamble.

"Had to go there first. Would you submit to Judge Cellini for me, please?"

"Already have," the man she called Jim responded. "I'll let you know when she signs off."

"Appreciate your help," Grace said shortly. She seemed to hesitate for a moment, then asked briskly, "Any movement on the Robinson case?"

"No. I had a call from McAvoy in Crimes Against Children. He wanted to know if he should take over since this turned into a possible homicide, but I put him off."

She sighed. "I should let him have it," she said, her shoulder slumping. "Lord knows I'm not getting anything on my end."

"You want me to give him a shout?" the other agent asked.

Grace shook her head. "Nah. I'm going to make a couple more calls and some more notes. If I don't shake anything loose in the next day, I'll call him myself."

"I'll get back to you as soon as we have the warrants. You have forensics people on standby?" the man on the other end asked.

"Ready and raring," she assured him. "Thanks again, Jim. I owe you."

Grace ended the call, dropped down onto the opposite end of the sofa and leaned over to jam the charger into a wall socket.

"He sounds pretty sure this other judge will issue the warrants," Matthew commented.

Grace's mouth pulled into a thin line. "Judge Cellini does a lot of work with victim advocacy groups in the Fort Smith area. Particularly female victims of abuse and violent crime. She'll issue the warrants."

"Good."

She plugged the other end of the cord into her tablet. "I'll pull the names from the firm's website, and you search for them on WhosIn. If someone has notifications set to show who's looking at their profile, they'll see another attorney and not the state police."

"Good call. This is why they gave you the shiny badge," he said, pointing at her. "Let's start headhunting."

Chapter Thirteen

The following morning, Grace dispatched the forensics teams she'd had standing by with warrants in hand. She'd set her sights on the target she and Matthew had agreed was the weakest link in the PP&W wall of silence.

Parking her SUV across the street from the law firm's front entrance, she scanned each car turning into the lot adjacent to the building. Her target sat too close to the steering wheel of a shiny eco-friendly hybrid. Taylor Greene appeared to be as uncertain about driving as she'd been about attending the previous day's meeting.

Grace switched off the ignition and climbed from the car. She crossed the street and the parking lot at a brisk pace, her head down so her hair provided some camouflage for her sneak attack.

Taylor hadn't even turned off her car. She rummaged around, gathering her belongings while she sang along with the music blaring inside the car. Grace cocked her head and hummed along until she picked up the thread of melody. Ms. Greene liked anthems of strength for young female empowerment disguised as pop songs. Duly noted.

She tapped on the driver's window with two knuckles. The young woman startled but turned instantly wary when she saw Grace.

Grace's eyebrows rose as Taylor turned down the volume and pushed the button to lower her window a scant few inches. "Sorry, I didn't mean to scare you." Grace tried to make her smile as friendly and unthreatening as possible. "One of my favorite songs."

Taylor Greene wasn't buying. She looked terrified, but Grace had to give her props for turning up the bravado when she asked, "May I help you?"

Grace flipped open her credentials as a courtesy. Okay, maybe it wasn't simply a courtesy. The badge and ID packed a wallop in certain situations. Still, she needed this woman's help, not a confrontation, so she kept her smile firmly in place, casual and friendly.

"I'm Grace Reed from the state police. We met yesterday?"

"Yes, I remember you."

Grace pocketed her badge. "I was hoping we could speak. You and I. Privately."

"I don't think that's a good idea—"

Grace saw her fumble for the button to raise the window and curled her fingers over the top of the glass to stop her. "Please. I know you were at the party Trey Powers hosted last Friday night. I need to talk to you some more about it, and I think we'd both prefer not to make a production out of it."

"How do you know if I was at the party?" the young woman asked, looking truly cornered.

Taylor wasn't as adroit as she should have been. "You were in pictures on social media."

The woman stared at her, aghast, as realization dawned. "You've been stalking me on social media?" she demanded. "You had no right—"

"No, ma'am," she quickly assured her, but she made a mental note to pay closer attention to Ms. Greene's accounts if they could gain access. "The photo was posted on Mallory Murray's PicturSpam account. I recognized you at the meeting yesterday, but I didn't want to say anything when there were so many—" she paused for a moment and leaned in "—guys around."

"I can't speak to you right now. I'm going to be late for work," Taylor said stiffly. "If you'll excuse me."

"I won't keep you long," Grace promised, stepping back slightly to make it clear she had no intention of boxing her in. "But a woman close to your age has died under what I think we can all agree are suspicious circumstances, and you were at the place where she was last seen alive."

Taylor Greene's already-fair complexion paled a shade.

"I was hoping you and I could talk privately. Of course, it's up to you if we speak in an official capacity. If you and your attorneys would like to meet me in, say—" she made a show of checking her watch "—an hour, I'm sure I can arrange a meeting room at the Benton County Sheriff's Department."

Taylor's gaze darted to the building. She shook her head quickly. "Listen, I went to a party, but I wasn't even invited personally. I sort of…ended up there."

"It shouldn't be a long conversation." Grace pulled yet another business card out of her pocket and passed it through the window. "I'm going to head to the coffee shop a couple blocks over. The Bean & Leaf? I need to pick up something to eat since I skipped breakfast." She smiled again and patted her stomach. "I wanted to catch you early if I could."

Grace hoped she came across as open and nonthreatening, but it was hard when you stood almost six feet tall. She needed a break, and if she could convince Taylor to talk to her, maybe they could turn the fissure in the PP&W facade into a crack. "If you haven't already had your morning coffee, maybe you'll stop by?"

Taylor took the card, but her hand fell to her lap, as did her gaze. "I can't make any promises."

"I won't ask you for any," Grace assured her. "I'm only looking for any information I can get to help me piece together what might have happened to Ms. Murray."

"I didn't know her," Taylor responded too hastily.

"Neither did I," Grace replied as she backed away another step. "But that doesn't mean she doesn't deserve justice, does it?"

Having delivered her message, Grace turned on her heel and walked back to her vehicle. When she slid in the driver's seat, she noted Taylor Greene still sitting in her car. She didn't appear to be talking to anyone or frantically texting. Choosing to read her lack of action as a good sign, Grace started the engine. If she hadn't run for the shelter of the PP&W offices by now, there was a chance she'd managed to snag her.

Wheeling her SUV out of the lot, she headed directly to the coffee shop. Her stomach gurgled. The part about skipping breakfast hadn't been a lie. Either way she'd get something out of this excursion.

She planned to text Matthew when she arrived at the coffee shop. When he'd left her hotel command center the previous night, he'd seemed bolstered by both the sandwich and their plan of action. She wanted to keep him in the loop as much as possible. His prosecutor's perspective was proving invaluable to her, and at this point, she needed every advantage she could get.

She took it as another good sign when a spot opened near the popular morning stop. Grabbing her bag, she headed inside the coffee shop. Like many of the businesses in the area, the interior was crammed full of rustic farmhouse decor. The thick soles of her shoes made no sound on the wide plank floor, but the place was buzzing.

A bottle of overpriced water and a cinnamon roll in hand, Grace made her way to the only open table—a tiny two-top crammed up against what appeared to be an old-fashioned pie safe. As she wound her way closer, she saw the owners had repurposed the cabinet to display packages of coffees and teas, mugs, and other kitschy detritus for caffeine junkies to purchase.

She tapped out a quick message to Matthew letting him know the team had been dispatched to the Powerses' lake house. Not wanting any distraction, she turned her phone facedown on the tabletop. She'd update Matthew on meeting with Taylor later. Hopefully, she'd have more to tell than a tale of accosting a young woman in a parking lot.

Stabbing the cinnamon roll with her fork, she glanced up surreptitiously whenever the bell above the door rang. She was only three bites into the gooey pastry when Taylor Greene walked in. But instead of going to the counter and placing an order, the younger woman made a beeline toward her.

She didn't take the open chair, though. Hovering near Grace's shoulder, she studied the rack of retail items. "This isn't a good place for me to talk," Taylor confided. "Tons of people from PP&W come here every day."

Grace nodded and turned to the window, paying no attention to the young woman standing next to her table.

"Name another spot," Grace answered, gathering up another forkful of the roll.

To her credit, Taylor hesitated only for a moment. "There's a place a few miles up the road in Springdale. It's called the Daybreak Diner. I've told the office I have to meet with a client this morning. I can meet you there in an hour."

Grace swallowed hard and gave a brief nod. "I'll be there."

Taylor looked nervous, and Grace felt for her. She was stuck between a rock and a hard place. Wanting to build rapport with this skittish witness, she cocked her to study the selection as well.

"I hear the sleepy-time blend is delicious," she said conversationally. If there was anyone from PP&W in there, she could make this meeting seem purely coincidental.

Taylor was quick to catch on. She wrinkled her nose and backed away, shaking her head. "I'm not much of a tea drinker, but I know somebody who is." She aimed a forced-looking smile at Grace. "Except the last thing I want him to be is sleepy."

Grace chuckled. "Totally understand. I can't begin to tell you which one would have the most caffeine."

She added a laugh so fake she wanted to take it back. Thankfully, Taylor rushed in to cover.

She waved a dismissive hand at the display. "He's more of the boil-a-bag type anyway. I probably shouldn't bother."

"If he's easily pleased, no sense in messing with a good thing," Grace concluded, then returned to the breakfast she no longer wanted.

Excitement made her stomach jittery. Without another word, Taylor turned to go, but something in Grace's gut told her Ms. Greene might be the wedge she needed to break this case wide-open.

The Daybreak Diner was the polar opposite of the Bean & Leaf. Instead of trendy reclaimed wood and metal signs meant to appear antique, the restaurant's interior was a genuine throwback to the 1980s. True to her word, Taylor sat in one of the brown vinyl booths spinning a heavy mug filled with coffee on the paper mat someone had placed beneath it to protect the table's Formica surface.

"Hey," Grace said, tossing her bag onto the bench opposite the younger woman. "Thanks for meeting me."

"I don't have long," Taylor returned, her voice snappish and her body language closed off.

"I'll get straight to it." Graced pulled her notepad and pen from her tote. "You said you weren't invited to the party yourself?"

"Coffee?" a waiter wearing a bored expression asked, already reaching for the mug he carried on a tray holding a half-filled carafe of black sludge.

Grace kept her gaze fixed on Taylor. "Water for me, please."

He turned away with a huff. Grace studied the other woman for any nonverbal cues. "Not invited…?"

"Well, no," Taylor conceded. "I was at Beaver Lake on a boat with someone else. We pulled into a slip alongside another boat, and the guys were talking back and forth. Trey said he was having a party at his family's place on Table Rock and pretty much invited everyone who was there."

"Who was there?" Grace asked as their waiter plopped a paper mat and glass of water down in front of her.

"Menus?" he asked, sounding even more uninterested than he had before.

"No, thank you," Taylor answered briskly. When he left again, she refocused on Grace. "I'd rather not give names."

Grace raised an eyebrow at the refusal. "Because you fear repercussions from PP&W?"

"Because the person I was with has nothing to do with who was at Trey's party," she parried.

"I bed to differ."

"He doesn't even work for PP&W."

Grace noted the pronoun slip. Taylor had said the "guys" were talking back and forth. A man. But whoever she was with was not one of the attorneys Steve had identified from the PP&W website.

"Why not share his name?" she asked, phrasing the question as neutrally as possible.

"Because I can tell you he had nothing to do with anything involving Mallory Murray."

"How do you know?"

"I know because he was with me."

"And you can't share his name because…?" When Taylor didn't answer, Grace was left to speculate. "He's clearly friendly with Trey Powers, but he doesn't work for PP&W. And you don't want to share his name because he's…involved with someone else?"

Taylor's head jerked back, but she raised her chin in stubborn defiance.

"Maybe married?" Grace pressed.

"I have to leave." Taylor moved to gather her purse.

"No, wait," Grace started to reach across the table, but paused prior to making contact. "I'll leave it. For now," she added under her breath. "What happened then? How did you get from Beaver Lake to the Powerses' place?"

"We got everything secured at the marina, then I rode with my friend."

"Is it normal to hop from lake to lake like that?"

Taylor shrugged. "I wouldn't say it's normal, but some people do it. I guess they get bored with what they have."

Grace picked up on the other woman's mild disapproval but didn't push. "And how did you end up at Stubby's Bar & Grill?"

Taylor's eyes widened for a moment, but she quickly masked her surprise. "Oh, Stubby's?" she said, sounding forced. "We were hungry. Everyone stops there after a day at the lake."

"You weren't worried about running into anyone who might know your, uh, friend there?" she asked, emphasizing the word.

Again, her pointed chin popped up. "He wasn't worried about it, so neither was I."

"Fair enough," Grace conceded. "I'm assuming y'all were playing follow the leader, since there were a few other people from PP&W."

"How do you know?" Taylor asked, not bothering to hide her surprise.

"Witness identification," Grace answered, noncommittal. "You and your new group of friends followed Mr. Powers to Stubby's Bar & Grill, where he started flirting with Ms. Murray," she ventured.

"I wouldn't say they were flirting."

"What would you say?" Grace asked, hoping to glean further insight from the lawyer's almost compulsive need to correct the facts as she knew them.

She shrugged. "Well, they clearly knew each other well. At first, I thought they might be a couple, but it's hard to imagine Trey dating someone like her."

"Someone like her?"

Taylor rolled her eyes and huffed a sigh. "Come on. She was pretty and all, but she was a waitress in a dive bar."

"You didn't think she was Mr. Powers's type," Grace determined.

"Not for something, you know, long-term. Frankly, I was surprised when he asked her if she wanted to come. The guys he was with weren't exactly polite to her."

"I see." She pivoted. "How long have you been with the firm?"

The change of tactic seemed to throw her. "Me? Three months. Why?"

"Only curious." She was fairly new. She might feel

her position with the firm to be vulnerable. "I assume you know Joshua Potter? He was with Mr. Powers that night, but I noticed he wasn't in the meeting yesterday. Why is that?"

She hesitated only for a moment but must have decided there was no use in trying to deny information Grace already had. "He's down in Little Rock , working on a case."

"Do y'all get called to Little Rock often?" she asked as she made a note on her pad.

"Actually, yes."

Taylor sat up a little straighter and tossed her dark hair over her shoulder. She clearly thought making a trek to the state capital inferred a level of prestige. The temptation to tell this innocent young woman exactly how often Grace made the trip herself was strong, but she resisted. Seeing a chance to pander to her ego, Grace ran with it.

"Must be a big case."

"We have a lot of important clients," Taylor replied.

"I bet."

"Senator Powers is Trey's uncle," she offered without segue.

Intrigued by the turn the conversation had taken, Grace looked up, happy to go along for the ride. "I think I heard that somewhere," she said mildly. "Does the firm do legal work for the senator?"

Taylor blinked as if the answer to the question was blatantly obvious. "Well, yeah."

Grace pounced. "And was Senator Powers at this party his nephew was hosting?"

"What? No," Taylor answered, shaking her head and

wrinkling her nose at the thought. "No, he's, uh, old. He wouldn't be at a party like this."

"A party like what?" Grace prompted.

"You know…a party. A party where people were partying… Young people." She finally ground to a halt there. "You know what? I do have to go now," she said, snatching up her purse and sliding from the booth in one fluid motion.

Grace followed suit, ignoring their server's shouts about their unpaid check as she followed Taylor into the parking lot.

"Hey, someone needs to pay," the waiter yelled from the open doorway.

Grace held up her badge and signaled for him to wait with one finger. She caught up to Taylor as she was opening her car door. Catching it in one hand, Grace held it open, allowing her guest to take a seat but preventing her from driving away. "Why didn't they send you to Little Rock, Taylor?" she asked. "Did they think you didn't know anything, or do they have something on you they know will keep you quiet?

"Your boyfriend is married, isn't he?" Grace tried the angle again, hoping to get a confession.

"Leave me alone. I have nothing left to say to you," Taylor said, trying to pull the door closed.

But Grace held firm. "Did they threaten you? Him?" Grace persisted. "Are you protecting him?"

"You don't understand," Taylor said, her voice breaking.

"But I do," Grace insisted, keeping her tone businesslike. "I understand a young woman is dead, and I believe you might know how it all happened."

Taylor began to cry in earnest but dashed the tears from her cheeks as fast as they spilled over. "I don't know, and you don't, either. You don't have any proof."

"I'll get the proof," Grace answered with a certainty she felt down to the soles of her shoes.

"It won't matter if you do. You know who they are. You know how connected the family is," Taylor said angrily. Gripping the steering wheel, she stared straight ahead as she whispered, "They'll ruin you."

"I don't care," Grace replied evenly. "I'll take them down with me."

"No, you won't."

"Did they tell you they'd trash your career if you told anyone what happened to Mallory Murray?"

"You don't know anything," she shot back, biting off each word. "Let me go. This conversation is over."

Seeing no advantage to turning a possible witness who might be wavering in her convictions into an adversary, Grace stepped back. "Thank you for meeting with me," she said as she released her hold on the car door.

Taylor slammed it shut without reply. Grace stood her ground as the other woman backed up without looking. She tore from the parking lot, crumbling asphalt flying from under her tires.

Grace drew a long breath and let it go slowly, taking a moment to let her brain catalog the bits and pieces she'd extracted from the encounter.

"You might be a cop, but someone still has to pay," their sullen waiter insisted, holding the diner door open wide.

Grace extracted a five-dollar bill from her bag and shoved it at the young man, who automatically grabbed hold of it. Turning on her heel, she jerked the strap of her tote onto her shoulder as she made for her car.

"Don't worry. I always make sure someone pays," she said, voicing her promise for all the universe to hear.

Chapter Fourteen

Matthew sat at his desk scrolling through his sister's PicturSpam account. Again. Looking at these photos had become some kind of obsession. Unable to sleep, he'd come in early and barricaded himself inside his office. So far, not one person had come tapping on his closed door, and he was grateful. It was enough to hear the bustle happening on the other side. He didn't want to be alone, but he didn't want to be a part of it.

He was only waiting for Grace to call and tell him he could come hide out in her war room again.

He scrolled through the images once more. He wasn't a social media guy, but he knew enough about the various platforms to understand he was only seeing a fraction of what Mallory had put out into the world. His sister loved to talk about herself too much to have posted fewer than a hundred photos on the world's most accessed platform.

His phone rang, and he glanced at the screen hoping to see Grace's name. Unfortunately, the call appeared to be coming from the coroner's office. Drawing a deep breath, he snatched it from the desk.

"Matthew Murray."

"Mr. Murray, this is Stu Mardle."

Matthew let the breath go slowly. He'd interacted with Stu on several occasions over the years. The prosecuting attorney often leaned on the county coroner to provide expert advice on cases beyond the results of routine autopsies. Matthew was fairly sure the medical examiner had never referred to him by his surname.

"Yes. Hello, Stu. I take it you have results?" he responded, hoping to make it clear he didn't expect the man to stand on ceremony just because Matthew was the victim's next of kin.

"I've forwarded my report to Special Agent Reed." Stu sighed. "Damn, Matthew, I couldn't *not* call you. I'm sorry for your loss."

"I appreciate you," he replied, his voice growing hoarse. "I don't suppose you have anything you can tell me?"

"You know how hard it is when a body is pulled from water. We're assuming she was there a few days or more."

"Which can slow any decomposition," Matthew interjected.

"And the clock sped up the minute she was on dry land again," the pathologist reminded him. "One thing we do know for certain is there was a blow to her head."

"With a flat object," Matthew said dully.

"Flat, smooth, but with some kind of divot or channel. A depression in the surface of some kind. Definitely not a log or anything rough. Some kind of finished surface." He paused. "I shouldn't say more than that until the agent from CID wants to release the information."

Matthew nodded his understanding, belatedly remembering the man on the other end couldn't see him.

"Yes. Of course," he said quickly. "I understand. I'm expecting to hear from Agent Reed soon."

"I'm sorry, Matthew. Helluva thing."

"Thanks, Stu. I appreciate the call."

After hitting the end button, he rocked back in his chair, the phone clasped in his hand. A smooth, flat object with a divot or channel. He swished his chair back and forth as he tried to stir his sluggish brain to life and come up with some ideas, but a thick, oppressive fog had descended on him.

The only thing he wanted to do was call Grace, but he couldn't. She had texted to say she had a meeting set up with Taylor Greene, and he didn't want to disturb her. But a text—he could send a text asking her to call as soon as she was available. He was trying to rouse himself enough to do just that when his office door flew open and Nate stormed in.

"Who the hell do you think you are?" he demanded without preamble.

Instinctively, Matthew curled the hand holding his phone into his chest. His boss stood in the now open doorway.

"She has no clue who she's messing with—"

He gaped at Nate's disheveled hair, mug-free hand and scowling expression. He'd never seen the man ruffled. Nor had he heard him angry. And he was upset about… Grace? The shroud of lethargy instantly lifted. He surged to his feet, unwilling to cede the position of dominance in his own office.

"Who does *who* think they're messing with?" he deflected.

"They have search warrants for the house and all the watercraft," Nate exclaimed.

Matthew stared at him, astounded by the consummate politician's sudden lack of self-control. Apparently he wasn't the only one. Nearly every lawyer and assistant in the open-concept office was practically falling out of their chair to get a better view of the floor show.

"Hey, take it down a notch," Matthew cautioned, making a tamping motion with his hand.

"I will not take it down a notch," the PA retorted, his voice rising to a shout. "I had Harold Dennis climbing straight up my backside, and I can tell you your name was mentioned more than once."

Matthew stepped forward, grasped Nate's arm and jerked him aside enough to swing the office door closed. The moment they were alone, he locked eyes with his boss.

"I don't care if Harold Dennis was using every letter of my name to spell out the numerous ways you're up *his* backside," Matthew hissed. "You're a damn prosecuting attorney. A crime has been committed. I don't know if you've forgotten, but you're supposed to be on the side of the law."

"Who says there's been a crime? You? The grieving *brother*?"

He said the last with heavy sarcasm, and it cut Matthew to the quick. Nate had hit the nail on the head. The brain fog? It was grief. Partnered with a few bonuses...like shock.

Disbelief.

Disillusionment.

He almost laughed when the last word popped into

his head. He'd thought he couldn't get any more jaded, but he was wrong.

"Mallory was struck from behind. The coroner's report has been sent to CID." He paused to take a shaky breath. "My sister was killed. She either fell or was dropped into Table Rock Lake. Someone left her there. Either way, a crime was committed."

"You have no proof Trey Powers is involved in any way," Nate persisted.

"We have proof the last place she was seen alive was at the Powerses' lake house. A judge seemed to think we had enough cause to search the place."

"I'd like to know which judge issued those warrants—" Nate began.

"I'm sure Harold Dennis can tell you. They do have to be signed, after all."

"No judge in three counties would dare—"

"Don't finish that sentence," Matthew ordered, holding up a hand.

To his credit, Nate stopped speaking. Matthew held his former mentor's gaze.

"I *am* a grieving brother," he said quietly. "I'm also a citizen. One who not only voted for you but also worked on your campaign. I'm not going to pretend I don't know who butters the bread around here. Please listen to me when I tell you I will not hesitate to report you to the bar if you do anything other than help the police convict whoever did this to Mallory. No matter who was involved."

He waited a beat, lifted a hand to Nate's shoulder and gave it a meaningful squeeze. "Are we clear?"

"Matthew, you don't understand—" Nate began, suddenly cajoling. Almost pleading.

"I do understand," Matthew shot back, letting his hand fall away. He spun around and scooped his laptop from his desk. Next, he snatched the messenger bag from the floor by its strap. "I understand better than you want me to," he said as he stuffed the computer into the bag.

Nate started to speak, but Matthew shook his head, emphatically insisting the other man remain silent. When Nate snapped his jaw shut, Matt would swear he heard the man's teeth clack.

"I'm going to take my bereavement leave starting now," he said quietly. Stepping past Nate, he opened the door. "I'm sure we'll be talking soon."

"Can you believe him?" Matthew cried, pacing the breadth of Grace's hotel room.

"Sadly, yes, I can," she murmured from her perch at the breakfast bar, her eyes glued to the screen of her tablet.

"Yeah, well, you don't know the half of what it's like to work with him day in and day out," he continued, refusing to let his rant be derailed by her inattention. "He wears shorts with the embroidered whales and anchors on them. What guy under seventy wears those?"

"Apparently one guy does."

At least she was replying on cue. Undeterred, Matthew paced the living area of the suite and unloaded all of it. "He has his teeth professionally whitened and likes to brag about the 'push presents' he gave his wife for each of their kids."

"Better have been diamonds," she said as she continued scrolling.

"For Hayden yes, but for Natalie she got a BMW. I guess she needed an SUV once they acquired the second kid and a Labrador."

"Nice."

Starting to get peeved by her lack of annoyance, he dug deep for something to set her off so they could hate on Nate together. "He only drinks tea."

"People say it's the house wine of the South."

"Not sweet tea, hot tea." He wrinkled his nose. "And not even real tea like the British, but the nasty 'stick a bag in the mug and drink some hot water that tastes like yesterday's socks' kind of tea."

"Ugh. Sounds awful," she mumbled.

Frustrated beyond words, he literally threw his hands in the air. "Okay, I give up. What the hell are you working on over there?"

At last, she looked up. "I'm going through the pathology report."

Matthew ran his hand over his face. "I told you what Stu said, right?"

"I think it was in there somewhere, but reading the report itself is much easier than trying to read between the lines of whatever you're going on and on about."

"I was trying to tell you my boss, the duly elected prosecuting attorney for this county, came into my office irate because I wasn't stopping you from investigating the death of a young woman who happens to be my sister."

"Yeah, but there was a lot of stuff about whales, tea parties and push presents. I stopped trying to sort it all out." She gave him a wan smile and tapped the screen of her tablet. "Your friend Stu is thorough but quite concise."

"Yeah, he is."

His sullenness must have seeped through to her, because she finally met his gaze.

"I'm sorry your boss is upset. But he's not my boss and I'm not afraid of these Powers people. The team is picking up fingerprints all over the boats, and I have a gut feeling we're on the right track." She paused and took a deep breath. "But I totally understand if you want to step back and stay out of the line of fire. You have your future to think about. I will see this through, I promise you."

"I don't want to step back," he said, markedly calmer. "I need to be a part of the solution."

"You need to let his anger roll off your back," she said, her eyes darting to her phone. "Ooh. Here's something to distract us."

"What is it?" he asked, craning his neck to peer at the message on the screen.

"I believe it may be the password for Taylor Greene's PicturSpam account."

"You know using illegally obtained information isn't going to hold up in court," Matthew warned.

"I'm not looking for evidence, Counselor. I'm looking for an angle. This girl feels like she is on the outside looking in at PP&W. I need to find a way to push those buttons."

She tapped away at her tablet until the screen filled with images posted with the handle @TGTigress95. She had started to scroll through them when another notification appeared. "Looks like she got into Mallory's as well. Do you want me to go through hers while you do Taylor's? There may be stuff on there a brother shouldn't see," she said, wrinkling her nose.

Matthew seemed to weigh his options. "Let's make a go at Taylor's first. We can deep dive on Mallory's if we see something to take us there. If you don't mind," he added, almost as an afterthought.

Grace shook her head. "Not at all." She nudged the tablet in his direction so they could both see the screen. "Bring the site up on your laptop and log in so we can compare one to the other if we need to."

"Sure." Matthew opened his sister's public profile. Grace leaned in and tapped in the username and password. Sure enough, hundreds more images loaded the moment she hit Enter.

"Jackpot," she murmured under her breath.

"Ho-ly," Matthew said in a shocked whisper.

Grace made a face as she cast him a sidelong glance. "What?"

"Nate," he replied, his face a picture of stunned disbelief.

She rolled her eyes, but her gaze tracked back to a beaming selfie Mallory had posted the night she disappeared. "Are you still babbling on about your boss?"

"No, I'm telling you this is Nate," he said, jabbing a finger her tablet.

Intrigued by the urgency in his voice, Grace followed his finger to a picture of a blond all-American-looking type with his arm slung around Taylor Greene's shoulder.

She squinted at the photo. "Didn't you tell me he was married?"

"He *is* married," Matthew confirmed.

"Definitely not separated or divorced?" she prompted.

Matthew shook his head adamantly. "He's a politician. He's as married as married can be. Two kids and a Labrador, remember? Push presents, a McMansion over in Hickory Hills and a gated subdivision near Beaver Lake."

Grace leaned over far enough to scroll through more of Taylor's photos. "Well, I'd say they appear to be more than friends." She frowned at another one of the photos. "How old is he?"

"Older than me. Thirty-eight? Thirty-nine?" Matthew reported.

"She's fresh out of school. Can't be more than twenty-six, though she looks much younger. How old are people when they finish law school?"

He shrugged. "Depends on if they go right into it. Direct from undergrad straight through to passing the bar, probably twenty-five unless they're some kind of prodigy."

"She's smart, but I don't think she's the skipping-multiple-grades kind of smart," Grace surmised. "She is naive, though. And I get the feeling she also has one of those pesky moral compasses most of you lawyer types lack."

"More of us have one than you think," he insisted.

"If you can introduce me to more than a handful, I'll buy the next pizza," she said as she continued flipping from photo to photo.

"Nate and this girl…"

"Wait." She stared hard at the photos, mentally replaying everything Taylor had told her about the friend she'd been out with that Friday night. "Does this Nate guy have a boat?"

"Of course he does." Matthew nodded. "Tons of people around here do, and not only people with money."

"I believe Ms. Greene was out on the boat with Mr.…." She paused long enough for him to pick up the cue.

"Able," he supplied. "Nathaniel Able."

"Mr. Able and Ms. Greene were out on his boat last Friday evening when they ran into Trey Powers and his friends, and Trey invited them to his crawfish boil."

"Friday," Matthew repeated. "I remember Nate saying something about his wife and the kids being at her family's beach house in Florida week before last. He took off early on Friday. Said he was going fishing."

"He caught something."

Grace sifted through photo after photo, scanning the background of each one for clues. She stared at the photo of the two people together as she rewound the conversation she and Taylor had in the first coffee shop. "Did you call him a tea drinker?"

"What?"

"When you were rambling on earlier, didn't you say something about Nate drinking tea?"

"You were listening?"

"I pick up all sorts of information from ambient noise."

"Yes, Nate drinks hot tea instead of coffee."

"Fancy tea or plain old bags?"

"The bag kind, why?"

"Confirming. I can tell you without a doubt Taylor Greene and your boss were involved in something more than a fling. At least, it's more on her side."

"Huh. Wow. I always thought Nate was a straight arrow." Matthew frowned. "He's a stickler for having things a certain way—making sure everyone dresses appropriately, keeping up appearances."

"Well, I doubt he was showing her off at fund-raising dinners," Grace said as she leaned closer to him to inspect the photos on the tablet she'd handed over.

"Do you want this back?" he asked, scooting it closer to where his laptop sat ignored.

"Hang on," she murmured. When she stopped scrolling, she tapped the screen. "There," she said, pointing to one of the last photos posted. It was of a group of people seated around an outdoor fire pit.

In the background, a well-lit dock provided access to four boats and a couple of personal watercraft. One of those boats was a sleek red ski boat with multiple wakeboards attached to the towing bar.

Inspired, Grace picked up her phone, opened her messaging app and tapped out a quick directive to the head of the forensics team asking how many wakeboards they'd found attached to the rack when they were on-site. A few minutes later, a message bubble appeared with the number four.

Grace snatched up the tablet, ignoring Matthew's grunt of protest as she opened the photo to full screen. She used her fingers to expand and refocus, homing in on the red boat. When she was finally able to zoom in on a clear shot of the ski boat, she blew out a low whistle.

"Three. There are only three wakeboards attached to the rack. Two on the driver's side, one over by where Mallory might have been standing."

"Conjecture, but I'll allow it," he said brusquely. "Where are you going with this?"

"Forensics found four attached to the rack when they reached the boat today. Two on each side."

"And the wakeboards are important because?" Matthew asked, trying to keep up. His frown morphed into a triumphant smile when at last he caught on. "They're objects with smooth, flat surfaces," he concluded.

"Do you know anything about wakeboards?"

"Yeah." He nodded slowly. "I've ridden them."

"Are they completely flat on the bottom, or do they have fins and—"

"Channels," he supplied in a whisper.

Grace snatched up her phone again, but she didn't bother typing out a message. She pressed the button to make a call.

"Hey, it's Grace Reed," she said when the person on the other end picked up. "I need you to pay special attention to the wakeboards. Particularly—" she leaned in and squinted at the photo, trying to make out the colors "—any board not painted black, blue or tie-dye-looking rainbow."

She let her gaze travel over all the details of the ski boat. If Trey were driving, Mallory would have stuck close to him. If he'd been driving after having a few drinks, she was likely hanging onto something. Had she been drinking? Maybe not if she knew she was pregnant. Had she leaned over the edge to vomit and lost her balance? Possibly, but that wouldn't explain the blow to the back of the head. But an unwanted pregnancy would.

"Closely examine the tow bar, the grab handle on the passenger side and maybe the dashboard. Anything somebody might have grabbed hold of for balance. Even the backs of the seats."

She listened in for a moment, then nodded. "Yes, let's concentrate on the ski boat first. I'm pretty sure she was on it."

She ended the call and placed her phone back on the bar. When she looked up, she found Matthew staring at her, horror etched into his handsome features.

"Someone hit her with a wakeboard," Matthew said, his voice hoarse.

"It's possible. Or she stumbled and hit her head against one mounted on the rack. Either way, I'm willing to bet she never made it back to the dock on Trey Powers's ski boat."

Chapter Fifteen

Matthew had thought the waiting was bad on the legal end of the system. Now, he realized he'd had no idea. Sure, juries deliberated for hours on end, and in one instance for days, but in those cases he hadn't had a personal stake in the outcome. He hadn't had to wait for a case to come together. When he got involved in a case, the police usually had things packaged up all neat and tidy.

It was eye-opening to discover how much Mallory's death was affecting him. In life she'd been an annoyance. He knew his sister had no ambitions beyond marrying well, but he supposed a part of him had hoped she'd find fulfillment in her role as a wealthy wife and mother. The possibility of the two of them finding some common ground was always out there.

It blew his mind to realize it would never happen.

In barely more than a week, everything had changed. Mallory had been alive and well and possibly scheming. And he'd been alive and well and wanting nothing do with her. What horrible, unthinking creatures people could be, he thought, rubbing a hand over his face. He'd been as selfish as she was in his own way. At best, self-absorbed.

He lay on the sofa in the sitting room of Grace's suite. For some reason, he couldn't force himself to go home. Eventually, she must have realized he was camped out, because she'd pulled a spare pillow and blanket off the shelf in the closet and handed them to him before heading into the bedroom.

Neither of them had made any mention of him going home. Nor had they made a plan for how to proceed once they knew for certain forensic evidence was available.

What was the deal with the car? His gaze traced nonexistent patterns on the ceiling. How had Mallory's car ended up in an entirely different lake?

If forensics came back with any kind of evidence placing Mallory on Trey Powers's boat, there was no way her vehicle had made it to Beaver Lake with Mallory behind the wheel.

Whoever had ditched it had been smart to lower the windows to be sure the vehicle was fully submerged. Most everything in it had either been ruined by water or washed away entirely. Whoever had done it had known how to compromise evidence.

Matthew sighed and swung his feet down from the sofa. His back popped as he leveraged himself into a standing position. It was going to be a long night, and he was parched. In the kitchenette, he refilled his empty water bottle from the tap. Water dripped onto his foot as he tipped it to his lips.

"Can't sleep?"

He jumped. The water missed his mouth and dribbled down his chin. He quickly swept it away with the back of his hand, whirling to find Grace standing behind him clad only in a set of striped cotton pajamas with drawstring pants an inch too short for her long legs.

Matthew stared at her bare feet, arrested by the pink polish he spotted on her toes when she covered one bare foot with the other.

He swallowed hard. "Huh? I mean, no." He winced. "Sorry if I woke you. I just wanted to get some water."

"I wasn't sleeping," she said, moving past him to pull a chilled bottle from the mini refrigerator. "And you don't have to drink from the tap if you don't want to. I have plenty in here." She pointed to the fridge with her unopened bottle.

"Tap works for me," he answered with a smile. "Never let it be said I'm a water snob."

"I won't," she replied somberly. "Aside from the obvious, anything running around in your head you want to offload?"

"Mallory's car—" he began, but she cut him off with an enthusiastic nod.

"Yeah, me, too. Someone else drove it to Beaver Lake."

He exhaled, relieved to know they were on the same page. "The spot where they dumped it isn't an obvious choice."

Grace walked over to the breakfast bar and looked at the list of names they'd been able to attach to faces on Taylor's and Mallory's photo feeds. "We can eliminate two of the guys we have on this list. The only one left would be Nate Able."

"And Taylor Greene." Matthew shook his head. "I still can't wrap my head around those two being a couple."

"It's possible they took the car together," she reasoned.

"And that would mean they were both witnesses to whatever happened to Mallory. I guess it sort of makes sense, aside from the fact it goes against everything they both swore to uphold," he mused.

"They both had a stake in keeping whatever happened quiet. Particularly Nate." Grace jabbed a finger at the photo of Taylor and Nate wrapped around one another. "He had everything to lose if their relationship came to light, and she had a lot to lose if she didn't keep whatever happened out on the lake quiet."

"I can't imagine believing a job is important enough to cover up a crime," he said, still trying to frame the theory in his head.

"I think we may have struck on why she's struggling. Pesky moral compass and all."

"That sounded sort of like a compliment," he teased.

She smiled but didn't take the bait. "I need to press Taylor harder," she thought out loud. "Question her like her presence was already a foregone conclusion. After all, they can't know for sure what forensics has or hasn't found. They may not even know the vehicle was pulled from the lake."

Matthew snorted. "Nate knows by now, I'm sure. And I'm willing to bet if he knows, Taylor knows. And let's face it, the people at PP&W will, too."

"There you go thinking they're omniscient again."

"Not omniscient, only highly connected," he corrected. "I agree, though. Taylor is the one to press."

Grace tapped the lid of her bottled water with a fin-gernail. "I'm going to check on the car first thing in the morning. See if there's any evidence of anyone other than Mallory in there."

"Good plan," he said, taking a fastidious sip from his own bottle.

"It's possible they'll find something."

Matthew appreciated her attempt at reassurance. He gave her a crooked smile. "Possible, but not probable. Either way, we can and will work with what we have."

She nodded. "Yes, we will."

"Thanks again for letting me hang out here. If I go home, I'm afraid my imagination will run even further afield. You're good at keeping me grounded."

Grace smiled and it lit a spark in her eyes. "Good night, Counselor," she said quietly.

"Good night, Grace."

She backed toward the bedroom door again. "I'll let you know if I get any information overnight. Otherwise, try to get some rest."

A second later she was gone, and the door clicked loudly in the silent room.

GRACE STOOD BESIDE the sofa in the suite's sitting room, torn. He looked so peaceful. Relaxed. She hated to wake him. Particularly when the news she had to give was of a grisly nature. But she wasn't here to watch this hand-some man sleep, she was here to catch his sister's killer.

She tried to wake him a gentle shake. "Hey."

Matthew tried to roll away, but he had nowhere to go. His nose ended up pressed to the back of the sofa. His grunt and groans of displeasure mirrored her own visceral reaction to having him turn away from her. Annoyed by the pang of wistful regret twisting in her belly, she gripped his shoulder and squeezed. Hard.

"Hey, wake up," she ordered, shaking him roughly.

"Ah, sheesh," he grumbled, batting her hand away. "Police brutality."

"We have a partial fingerprint."

His eyes flew open, and he sat bolt upright. "Mallory's?"

"No, the pope's," she returned, spinning away from him. "Yes, Mallory's. On one of the grab bars on Trey Powers's boat," she called over her shoulder. "Give me a minute to finish getting dressed. We're heading down to the sheriff's department. I asked them to hold a room for me. We'll meet with the head of the evidence-receiving team there."

"I need coffee," he called after her. "And we'll have to swing by my place. I need to shower and change."

Grace snorted. "You'd better get moving, because I can be out of here in less than two minutes."

After a drive-through coffee run, they made a quick pit stop at his apartment for Matthew to freshen up. The drive to the county sheriff's offices took fifteen long, tense minutes.

"I'm glad they built this out here and not by the courthouse," Matthew said as they turned into the sprawling complex on the west side of town.

"Convenient to have the offices attached to the detention center," she said, eyeballing the razor wire–topped fence enclosing the back of the property.

"With the way things are growing up here, they couldn't keep everything downtown."

"Makes sense."

They parked and walked into the building, Matthew clutching an enormous to-go cup.

Mark Atkins, the receiving officer from the Department of Public Health's State Crime Laboratory greeted them in a windowless meeting room off the main hallway.

After handshakes were exchanged and introductions made, Grace leaned in. "I know it's unusual to have a member of the victim's family on hand at this stage, but Mr. Murray is the assistant prosecuting attorney for Benton County and grew up in the area. His expertise has been instrumental smoothing the way for this investigation."

Atkins's bushy eyebrows rose. "Judging by the house, the boats and the number of lawyers who showed up to oversee the search, it looks like you've had to do a lot of smoothing. We don't usually have such an, uh, attentive audience when we do our thing."

"Yes, well, I'm pretty sure I'm never going to make it onto the Powers family's Christmas card list," Matthew said dryly.

Grace dropped into one of the molded plastic chairs. "What have you got for me?"

"Two things at this point," Atkins reported. "Of course, these are preliminary findings, and everything we've found—both on the scene and in the vehicle—has been sent to the lab in Little Rock for further confirmation."

"Of course," Grace confirmed.

"We picked up a clear partial print from one of the grab bars. Comparison in the mobile lab shows it to be a match for your, uh..." He broke off, glancing at Matthew with uncertainty.

"Victim," Matthew supplied gruffly.

"Yes, victim," Atkins continued.

He showed them a screen capture of fingerprint whorls on his tablet. Matthew peered over her shoulder when he passed the tablet to Grace. She was no expert, but it looked like a match to her. Still, evidence of Mallory's presence on the boat didn't give them anything concrete. She might have gone for rides on the lake with Powers every weekend, for all they knew.

After Grace and Matthew had both examined the image, she placed the tablet in the center of the table. "Any hair?"

"Yes, quite a bit. Too much to differentiate at the scene," Atkins answered with an apologetic grimace.

She was about to ask the big question when he stopped her with a brisk nod.

"There were strands of hair collected from one of the boards attached to the rack, though." Again he sent an apologetic glance at Matthew. "We bagged the whole board, but I'd estimate the strands to be between sixteen and eighteen inches long."

"And what color was the board?" Grace asked.

Atkins's expression was a bizarre mixture of triumph and distaste. He was exultant to have found something, but also disgusted by what the evidence might mean.

"This board was red and black. Glossy finish, not as long as the others."

He slid a finger across the tablet, and a photo of a red wakeboard in a large evidence bag filled the screen. "It measures less than seventeen inches wide."

They were looking at the top of the board, where a rider would attach to bindings. "Do you have other angles?"

"Yes." He swiped again, and slightly curved edges of the board were shown. The next was a photo of the bottom of the board. Small tail fins anchored one end, and two shallow channels ran the length of the board.

The next photo showed the board attached to the tow bar. It was large bar that formed an arch behind the driver and passenger seats, almost sectioning off the open seating and the deck at rear of the boat.

"Mallory wasn't short," Grace mused as she flipped through the photos again. "It's possible she could have fallen backward and hit her head on one of the wake-boards."

Matthew and Atkins nodded along, but Matthew interjected. "But the red board would not have been mounted on the rack. The photos from that night only showed the other three boards."

Grace nodded. "True."

She puzzled over the forensic photos again, fumbling to pull her own tablet from her bag. The picture posted on Taylor Greene's PicturSpam feed popped up the moment she opened the app. She used her fingers to zoom in again, needing to be sure she hadn't imagined there were only three boards attached to the rack.

"No. There were only three that night, and only one on the side of the boat where Mallory might have been standing." She passed Atkins his tablet back.

"All of this needs to be verified at the lab. I'll be sure to be in contact with you as soon as I get anything," the forensics expert assured her.

"I appreciate you staying behind to talk to us for a few minutes." She nodded to his tablet. "Would you mind sending those to me?"

The other man hesitated for a moment. "I shouldn't. Once we have confirmation about the prints and can identify the hair found on the board, I can send you official photos, but I shouldn't give you anything until then."

Grace gave a hum of disappointment but offered a knowing smile. "I understand."

They'd moved to gather their belongings when Atkins leaned over and tapped at the bottom of his screen. A second later, a request to receive files via Bluetooth connection appeared on Grace's tablet. She accepted without saying a word.

"I appreciate you staying to give us what information you could." Grace held his gaze as they shook hands.

"It's my pleasure, Agent Reed." He turned to Matthew. "My condolences on your loss, Mr. Murray." With a nod, Mark stepped past them and left the windowless meeting room.

Matthew dropped back down into the plastic chair with a heavy thud. "She didn't stumble back into those boards."

"As you pointed out, this particular board wasn't there to stumble into."

Grace took her seat again, and together they went through the photos Atkins had shared with her. "Even if it comes back as a match for Mallory's hair, it's going to be hard to prove intent."

"Yes, it will."

"But hope is not lost," Grace murmured as she double-checked to be sure the pictures were saved to her photo roll.

Turning to the man beside her, she cocked an eyebrow. "It may not be easy, but it's not impossible. We know there were witnesses. We know who those witnesses were. All we need is to get one crack and the rest will fall into place."

"Do you think she'll crack?" Matthew asked.

Grace didn't need a name to know which she he meant. "I think she's our best bet."

"They're not going to let you near her unguarded again."

"You think I'm scared of a bunch of suits?" The Powers team were not the kind of attorneys who hustled up work by advertising on billboards. They drew the cream of the crop. They had every weapon at their disposal.

Money.

Power.

Influence.

And, most important, leverage.

But they wouldn't be toting actual weapons into the conference room. At least, she hoped not.

"You know they're going to drag your boss down with them," she said, watching his face to see exactly how the statement landed.

"I know."

"There will be some who will say you're pursuing this to create a vacuum in the prosecuting attorney's office."

Matthew gave an incredulous bark of laughter and stared at her in bemused amazement. "Are you serious?"

She gave a helpless shrug.

"You think people will believe I had my sister killed

by the son of one of the area's most influential families in order to bring down my boss so I can slide into this job?"

Grace chuckled at his assessment. "I'm not saying its believable, but there will be people who will twist this story every which way but loose. You need to be prepared for fallout."

"I wasn't prepared to have my sister disappear only to find her body in a lake days later, yet here I am, still functioning."

"True."

"They can come at me if they want. You're the one who keeps telling me I've got this damn moral compass," he added, pinning her with a glare.

Grace nodded and began to pack her things into her tote bag. "Come on. Let's give them their room back. We'll head to the suite, where we can talk in private. I need to figure out the best way to finagle an appointment to see Taylor Greene."

As they were leaving the Benton County detention center, Grace's phone rang. She pulled it from her bag and scowled when she saw Ethan Scott's name on the screen. She immediately accepted the call.

"Hey, Chief, what's up?" she asked, trying to tamp down the tension rising inside her.

"I need to talk to you about Treveon Robinson," her boss said without a greeting, and her stomach dropped to her feet.

She hadn't thought about Treveon for one minute since she told Jim Thompson not to hand over his case, and now Chief Scott was calling her. Grace realized with a jolt she was no better than anyone else—she'd put the boy's disappearance out of her mind while she pursued a bigger, juicier case.

Chapter Sixteen

Grace halted in her tracks. She'd failed him. She'd failed Mallory. Why hadn't she done more to find him sooner? She must have looked as thrown as she felt, because Matthew's eyes widened in concern.

"Where?" she asked, needing to hear the answer she dreaded, no matter how much it would hurt.

"He was spotted in a Texarkana shopping center. Someone took down the information on the car. When police got there, he was with a man who claimed to be his father," he reported.

Treveon was alive.

She couldn't speak. Relief and fury warred inside her. Treveon's mother had sworn up and down the boy's father wasn't involved in his life, though they had been married. It was possible no crime had been committed at all.

"The local child services department has him in their custody now. I'm turning this case over to Crimes Against Children. They'll sort out the custody question, and they can get the Bureau involved if indeed it turns out to be kidnapping."

"Oh… Okay. Thank you for letting me know, sir."

"Well, you were hot on this one when you caught the Murray case, but now you are free to focus your energies entirely on what you have going there."

"I appreciate the call. Thank you."

The news Treveon was safe and well should have elated her, and it did. Sort of. But cop emotions were often the opposite of what her sister termed "real people" emotions. She'd put Treveon on the back burner, and now someone else was going to be the one to deliver him back to his mother. And she was disappointed about it. How messed up was she?

"Anything happening with your investigation there?" her boss asked.

Grace turned in a slow circle, taking in her surroundings. "I'll call you from a more private location with an update," she promised him, careful to keeping her voice neutral and businesslike. "The quick and dirty is, I'm waiting on more concrete information from the crime lab."

He replied he'd be expecting her status report, and she ended the call.

"What is it? What happened? You went white as a sheet," Matthew persisted, barely giving her a second to breathe. "Is it Powers? Did they try to shut things down?"

"Not everything is about this case," Grace snapped. He blinked in shock, and she gritted her teeth. "Sorry. Another case."

"I gather." He gestured for her to start walking again.

"Something I was working on when—"

"No need to explain," he said, cutting her off. "Let's go."

"I—"

He stopped and stared straight into her eyes. "I understand."

The funny thing was, she knew in her gut he truly did. They were alike, she and Matthew. Both driven to do their best by the people counting on them. She wasn't about to let off the gas now.

"I'm going to meet with Taylor Greene," she announced as she set her sights on the parking lot. "It's time to apply pressure."

GRACE AND MATTHEW sat in the same plush leather executive chairs they'd occupied on their last visit to PP&W. The difference was, they'd been left alone in the room and had been for at least fifteen minutes.

"You think they're messing with us?" she asked, checking her watch again.

"Undoubtedly. Plus, I assume they're doing some strategizing."

They'd arrived at the PP&W office unannounced. Grace had flashed her badge and informed the receptionist she needed to see Mr. Trey Powers, Ms. Taylor Greene and Mr. Joshua Potter as soon as possible. Without asking permission, she marched into the conference room with a full head of steam.

"I wonder if Joshua Potter will magically be teleported back from Little Rock," she mused.

"I doubt he ever left town."

Tipping her head back, she stared up at the ceiling. "If you were Mallory, where would you have stashed the stick?" she mused aloud.

"The what?"

"Never mind. I was thinking about the other test,

but not now," she said, pitching her voice low but not bothering to mask her impatience.

"Oh. I was hoping it would turn up in her car, but no luck there."

Grace heaved a sigh. They'd received a call on their way across town. Mallory's purse had been found locked in the trunk, but the compartment had flooded. Her wallet survived, but her driver's license was not in it. And, sadly, there'd been no sign of the second pregnancy test.

Matthew suspected she'd had her license and the test in the console of the car or on her person, but Grace wasn't sure. If she had something she thought might turn out to be her golden ticket, the first thing she would do would be to lock it up somewhere no one else could access. Like a bank box or a safe.

"What are the odds she had a safety-deposit box?" she asked.

Matthew snorted a laugh. "I'd say slim. She had at least two banks shut down her checking accounts for excessive overdrafts."

"Hmm." Grace tapped her pen against the pad of paper in front of her. "She would have put it someplace safe. Someplace no one would think to look." She twisted her chair back and forth as she thought. "Not at the apartment, not in her car—"

"We hope," Matthew interjected.

"Not on her person," she continued, letting her mind wander to all the places a woman might stash something valuable only to her. Her thoughts instantly traveled to the center drawer of her desk at the Fort Smith office, where she kept her father's old badge as both a talisman and a reminder. "Could she have hidden it at Stubby's?"

"Stubby's?" Matthew asked, surprised by the notion. "Why?"

She shrugged. "Maybe she wanted to see how Trey responded to the news first. For all we know, he's been violent or threatened her in the past. Your sister seemed to be cautious with people. She kept her roommate at arm's length, and there was barely anything personal at her place. Maybe she had reason not to trust Trey completely?"

"But she'd trust Steve," he said, almost to himself. "If not him personally, she might be willing to risk leaving something on the premises. She'd worked there for years."

Grace murmured to herself as she made a note on her pad. "Check Stubby's."

As she was drawing and redrawing a box around the word, Matthew's phone buzzed, dancing across the polished mahogany surface of the conference table. Grace opened her mouth to give him some grief for leaving it on when she felt her own vibrate in her suit pocket. Exchanging sheepish smiles, they both reached for their devices.

"This will be when they come in," she mumbled as she unlocked the screen.

"Huh," Matthew huffed, reading his message. "Apparently, I'm committing career suicide today."

He turned the phone to show her the message from Nate Able.

"Already alerted to our presence," she said, affecting an impressed nod. "Bets on whether it was Taylor or someone higher up tipping him off?"

He waved the offer away. "Either way I lose, right?"

"Right."

Grace's mood turned grim. Matthew did have more to lose by being here, but when she'd suggested he stay behind, he'd told her she'd have to cuff him to the car. She'd actually considered it for a moment. It was one thing for her to beat the hornets' nest, but she didn't have to deal with these people once she sewed up this case. Matthew had plans for a life here.

Looking down at her own phone, Grace let out a bark of laughter when she saw the message. Sure enough, the chief had sent a warning she'd ticked off the head honcho. He instructed her not to leave without the goods.

Right on cue, the conference room door swung open and an imposing man with Trey's handsome features and silver streaks in his perfectly barbered hair strode in.

She and Matthew stood. He had the sort of presence that commanded it. Trey followed a pace behind the man, and trailing him were a good dozen or more suits, each clutching their own pens, pads or portfolios.

"Tyrone Powers," the older man said, extending a hand to Grace. "And you are Special Agent Grace Reed."

"Yes, sir," she replied respectfully.

"I've heard you're quite tenacious, Agent Reed," he said, giving her hand another squeeze.

She was about to respond, but the man had already turned his spotlight on Matthew. "Mr. Murray. I am sorry about your loss," he said as they clasped hands. "Too young. Such a shame."

Following directly behind his father, Trey gave them a perfunctory hello and handshake. Grace noted he appeared considerably less cocky than he had in their previous meeting.

She watched as the other lawyers filled in around the table, leaving the two chairs opposite Grace and Matthew open. Sure enough, the father and son laid claim to them. A tall, thin man with floppy dark hair who matched the headshot they'd identified as Joshua Potter sat on Grace's far right. Taylor Greene sat at the opposite end of the conference table. For a moment, she wondered if the seating arrangement was purposeful.

"Thank you for meeting with me," she began, addressing the room in general. "I admit I wasn't expecting to have such a large audience."

"While we appreciate the gravity of what happened to Ms. Murray, the associates at Powers, Powers & Walton do not have unlimited time to answer questions about somebody they'd met at a single social occasion," Harold Dennis began stiffly.

Tyrone Powers reached over and pressed a staying hand to his attorney's forearm. "Hal, a young lady is dead," he said in a drawl as soft and genteelly Southern as a character in a Tennessee Williams play. "I know Special Agent Reed would not be here if she didn't feel it was necessary."

Grace and Matthew exchanged a glance. It was clear the elder Powers and his counsel had decided who was going to play good cop in this scenario. But Grace was the only real cop in the room and could play the game better than either of them.

"Absolutely not, sir," she agreed briskly. "It's come to

our attention that Ms. Murray may have been involved in a relationship with someone at the party. This relationship," she continued, choosing her words with extreme care, "might have been one some people would consider a sensitive subject."

"Sensitive how?" Harold Dennis asked.

"A secret relationship, sir," Grace said, politely pouring on her own brand of Southern charm.

"A secret relationship," Tyrone Powers repeated, sounding mildly amused. "Definitely intriguing. Do go on, Agent Reed. Who do you believe was involved in this 'secret' relationship?"

Beside him, Trey cringed as his father crooked his fingers to simulate air quotes.

Grace made a point of glancing at the array of attorneys situated around the table. "Once again, I think it might be better for everybody involved if we were to have this conversation with only the individuals who attended the party."

"Not going to happen," Harold Dennis replied tartly. "Ask your questions, Agent Reed. These people are busy, and you can't afford our hourly rate."

"True," Grace said with a smile. "Certainly not on a state government salary."

She glanced over at Matthew, who gave an almost imperceptible nod. They'd practiced the move in the car. Multiple times. She'd wanted it to appear he was giving his blessing to asking the uncomfortable questions, but not without some reservation.

"I believe Mallory Murray was attending the party as the guest of Nathaniel Able."

Grace heard Taylor's sharp intake of breath but forced

herself not to turn in the young woman's direction. She wanted Taylor to see exactly how quickly the men around this table would throw her lover under the bus if it meant saving one of their own.

"Nathaniel Able?" Tyrone Powers asked, his tone indicating he was truly shocked. "Nate?" He shifted his gaze to Matthew. "Nate Able, the prosecuting attorney for Benton County? Your boss?"

Matthew did nothing more than open his hands in a gesture of futility. "My sister is dead, Mr. Powers. I want answers."

Harold Dennis spoke up, picking each word he uttered carefully. "Do you have evidence of such a relationship?"

"We have evidence of a relationship. Mr. Able has not been particularly circumspect with regard to honoring his wedding vows," Grace said, choosing her words with equal care.

"Oh, well—" Tyrone Powers let the thought hang there as he glanced over at his son. "Did you know Nate Able was having an affair?"

Grace had to admire the older man's acumen. He'd asked his son a direct question, but not one specific enough Trey would have to lie in order to answer it.

"Yes, sir."

Tyrone nodded and swallowed. His grimace told her he found this particular admission distasteful. "I see. And you allowed this…affair to carry on at our family home on the lake?"

Grace wanted to sit back and watch this farce play out, but she had to keep pushing. She needed to see exactly how much it would take for the Powers men to pin Mallory's death on Nate Able. She wasn't certain how far she would have to go to make Taylor Greene break ranks.

"To be honest, sir," Trey began, addressing his father respectfully, "I invited Nate to the party, but I didn't realize he'd be bringing a date along."

Grace did her best to keep her features neutral. She could almost feel the panic bubbling up inside Taylor. A surge of raw energy emanated from her side of the room like a wave of sound carrying across water. The others must have felt it, too, because she caught more than a few confused glances exchanged between the assembled attorneys.

"Agent Reed, I hope you understand neither my wife nor I condone such behavior," Tyrone Powers said smoothly. He shot his son a sidelong glance she assumed was meant to be censorious. "And I certainly don't approve of my son providing a forum for such behavior."

"I'm not here to pass judgment on your family, Mr. Powers," she said stonily. "I'm only here to get to the bottom of what might have happened to Ms. Murray. We don't believe her death was an accident."

"Has the coroner given a probable cause of death?" Harold Dennis cut in.

She nodded, though she was fairly certain the Powers team already had access to the coroner's report. "Ms. Murray sustained a blow to the back of her head. It appears someone struck her from behind. She either fell or was pushed into the water."

The people sitting opposite them absorbed this information with a disturbing lack of reaction, but Harold Dennis did cut a glance in the direction of Taylor

Greene, and even Grace could read the warning in the older man's icy stare.

"There are at least three people in this room, maybe more, who we can confirm were there Friday night. We're hoping as officers of the court, you will come forward to bear witness to what actually took place," she said, staring directly at Joshua Potter.

The young man wagged his head in vehement denial. "I was there that night but spent most of the evening hanging out by the fire pit. I was talking to a girl I knew from school and, you know…" he trailed off with a shrug. "I don't like boats."

"He was hitting on Ainsley Markham again," Trey chimed in.

"And getting shot down again," Chet Barrow, Trey's budget doppelgänger, added, not bothering to mask his mockery.

"I see." Grace scribbled the words *no Josh* on the pad in front of her. She looked at the young man who clearly wished he were the heir to the Powers fiefdom. Knowing it would likely provoke him, she asked, "I'm sorry, I know we were introduced, but what was your name again?"

The young lawyer sat up straighter, noticeably offended by not being remembered. "Barrow. Chet Barrow."

Grace flashed him her sweetest smile. "Yes, I remember now." She zeroed in on him, her eyes narrowing as she used the cocky young man to push poor Taylor Greene closer to the edge. "You seem to be an observant man, Mr. Barrow. I think we can all agree Ms. Murray was an attractive young woman. Surely you saw her at the party with Mr. Able, didn't you?"

"I, uh…" He glanced at Trey, then at Tyrone Powers, who gave an encouraging nod. "I saw them there."

"You saw them there together," Grace pushed for clarification.

His gaze returned to Trey, who sat staring back at Grace, his expression impassive. Finally, Barrow nodded enthusiastically. "Yes. She and Able seemed to be pretty hot and heavy. I assumed Trey was doing them a favor by making such a show out of inviting her to the party. I mean, she's a waitress in a bar, right?"

"Right," she replied mildly.

His misogyny and plain old-fashioned snobbery had Grace seething inside, but she knew in her gut it wouldn't take much more to make Taylor Greene erupt. She was winding up another shot at Nate when Barrow piped in again.

Clearly warming to the spotlight, he forged ahead with the lie. "And everyone knows old Nate is kind of a dog when it comes to women. Not picky, if you know—"

"He is, too!" Taylor Greene burst forth.

All heads swiveled in her direction. At last, Grace turned to find the diminutive brunette had shot to her feet. Her fists were clenched, and her eyes blazed.

"Excuse me?" Harold Dennis asked coolly, his jaw set hard.

But Taylor was beyond caring. "He is not a dog. He has impeccable taste!"

Grace chanced a quick glance at Matthew. "What makes you say so, Ms. Greene?" Grace asked, sounding no more curious than someone asking how her day was going.

"Because *I* am the one who is having an affair with Nate Able. *I* am the woman he brought to the party." Her voice trembled when she spoke, but Grace instantly recognized it shook from rage, not fear. "They're lying." She spat the word. "They have to lie because everyone knows he did it. Everyone knows he's the reason she's dead."

Both Tyrone and Trey Powers began to speak at once, Tyrone in a placating voice, while his son's was decidedly more disdainful. But it was Harold Dennis who barked the order for the insubordinate junior associate to take her seat and stop speaking.

To her credit, Taylor did neither.

"Everyone knows *who* did it? *Who* is the reason?" Grace prompted, her gaze fixed on Taylor.

"I told you," she said, turning on Grace. "I told you about me and Nate. You know they're lying."

"I need you to tell me what happened to Mallory," Grace replied, calm and even. "Who did what?"

"Ms. Greene," Tyrone Powers said sternly as he rose from his chair.

She blinked, then looked at Trey's father imploringly. When she spoke, her voice was barely more than a stunned whisper. "He left her there. *He*…left her there. Like she was nothing more than a piece of trash."

Chapter Seventeen

Vitriol. Matthew had heard a lot of nasty things said about victims in the past, but seldom did he hear such vehement denials and denunciations of both Mallory and Taylor as he did in the sixty seconds after Taylor Greene's whispered accusation.

He let the words roll over him for a minute more, absorbing some of their impact as his due. After all, he'd said similar things about Mallory.

"Scheming—"

"Liar, you didn't see anything—"

"Why he would bother with anyone like you—"

"Your career is over, young lady. I will personally see to it no firm in this state—"

And so it went. Matthew didn't even bother trying to track who was saying what. He was too focused on watching Trey Powers.

The other man sat silent and still, his mouth clamped shut tight. A muscle ticked in his jaw, but he didn't speak another word.

Beside him, his previously serene father had turned into a whirlwind of bluff and bluster. Chaos reigned in the room, and only he, Grace and Trey seemed to stay above the fray. Or rather, below it, because everyone else had leaped from their chairs to start shouting over one another.

"My son was not involved with that woman," Tyrone Powers bellowed.

Everyone fell quiet then, and Matthew dragged his attention from the son to the father. The elder Powers looked flustered—his neck and face florid above the collar of his white-on-white-striped collar and his hair falling onto his forehead.

"He was," Taylor Greene shouted back, heedless of the sudden silence enveloping the room. "They were together. And it wasn't a new thing. I saw the way they looked at each other. I saw the way they were talking at the party, all close and intense. Something was going on between them."

"You're fired," the older man said bluntly. "Get the hell out of my office."

"Now, Ty—" It was Harold Dennis's turn to try to smooth the waters.

But Taylor Greene was done. "You know what? Fine." She snatched her portfolio from the table and took a stumbling step back. "I'm done with the lies. I'm done with all of it."

"Ms. Greene, I'm afraid the terms of your employment agreement—" Dennis began.

The young woman snorted. "My employment agreement?" she asked derisively. "Where is the part about covering up murder written into my agreement?"

Grace rose to meet the young woman face-to-face. "Did you witness the assault on Ms. Murray?"

Matthew tried to get up, too, but couldn't get his feet under him.

"There's no proof. My client—" Mr. Dennis tried again.

Matthew watched as Grace crossed to Taylor Greene and looked the young woman in the eye, but she kept her voice pitched too low for him to hear what she said.

"You knew!" the younger woman cried. "Why should I tell you anything? You used what I told you for leverage. You pushed and pushed until…oh my God." Her gaze flew to Tyrone Powers once more. "I didn't mean to. I… I needed to protect Nate. What she was saying about Nate and that Mallory woman was not true."

"Did you witness Mr. Powers harming Ms. Murray?" Grace asked again, the pointed question cutting through various conversations.

Matt turned his attention back to Powers, interested to see how the question played out on the man who had clearly believed himself to be untouchable up until this moment. But Trey, with his father's hand planted firmly on his shoulder, remained mute.

"What cause would my client have to do such a thing?" Harold Dennis blundered on.

"You have no proof Ms. Murray was harmed while in Mr. Powers's company," Michelle Fraser interjected coolly. "You have no motivation."

Matthew felt compelled to speak. "I can tell you without a qualm we have enough evidence to arrest at least four people in this room today." He spoke quietly enough that the raised voices around him fell away.

Heads swiveled to Harold Dennis, and the other man stilled. "On what charges?"

"Operating watercraft under the influence?" He tossed it out like a fishing hook into chum-baited waters. The other man, nonplussed, couldn't respond. "Or leaving the scene of an accident?" He raised a hand and pointed in Taylor Greene's general direction, his eyes still locked on Trey. "She said you did."

"One unfounded accusation doesn't mean—" Michelle Fraser began.

"Assault? Aggravated assault? Reckless endangerment? Those are all possibilities, and we haven't even gotten to intent. Intent opens up a lot of other possibilities." He shifted his gaze to one after the other. "And I'm sure as officers of the court, all your friends know there's a whole menu of possible charges waiting for them, too. Failure to report an accident, obstruction of justice, possibly even tampering with evidence? Any of those sound like a good fit?" he asked, glancing over at Grace.

"Sky's the limit," she replied coolly.

"Literally," Matthew said, the word dry as dust. "Don't forget, Table Rock Lake is considered a federal waterway. There could be a whole slew of federal charges facing whoever was involved."

"True," Grace confirmed.

He turned his attention back to Trey. No one moved. No one spoke. An unnatural silence filled the room.

"Frankly, I'm leaning more toward murder, but I may be biased," he said, holding the other man's gaze. "Premeditation is the big question."

Mr. Dennis recovered first, but when he spoke, the words came out hollow. "You have no reason to believe—"

Matthew ignored him, his eyes narrowing on Trey. At last, the other man broke, shifting his attention to Tyrone Powers. He clearly expected his daddy could save him.

"When did Mallory tell you she was pregnant, Trey?" Matthew asked, his voice lethally quiet.

The elder Powers flinched, but the younger went stock-still, like an animal who knew he was caught in the hunter's sight line.

"Do not answer any questions," Ms. Fraser interjected.

"Did you know she was pregnant when you came to Stubby's? When you took her out on your boat?" Matthew persisted.

"Pregnant?" Ty Powers asked, turning a befuddled gaze at his son.

Ignoring counsel's advice to keep his mouth shut, Trey turned to his father. "If she was, it's not mine," he said imploringly. "I hadn't seen her in almost two months."

"But you don't deny having intercourse with her," Grace said, moving back to her spot and planting her hands firmly on the conference table. "You and Ms. Murray have had sexual relations."

"Yeah, but—"

Trey's protests were cut off by Michelle Fraser's shout. "Shut up. Now!"

In the residual silence, Grace picked up her cell phone.

"Everybody back to their offices immediately," Harold Dennis barked.

"No," Grace retorted. Holding her phone in her left

hand, she stepped in front of the conference room doors. Matthew gawked at mulish set of her chin as she raised the phone to her mouth. "I'm going to need you all to stay here, please."

"You can't—"

But Grace wasn't listening to anything more Harold had to say. Instead, she switched her phone to speaker mode. "Sheriff Stenton?" she asked when a gravelly voiced man answered.

"Yes, ma'am."

"This is Special Agent Grace Reed of the Arkansas State Police," she said, her gaze locking first with Harold Dennis, then skimming over Tyrone Powers and landing on his son. "Is the backup and transport I requested earlier ready?"

"Yes, ma'am. We're right outside."

Grace nodded. "Please, come in. I'll have at least four detainees, and I imagine each of them is going to want to lawyer up separately."

She ended the call, then asked the room in general, "Is there anyone here who needs me to remind them of their Miranda rights?"

Matthew rose and went to stand next to her. "How can I help?" he asked.

She leaned over and whispered, "You might want to give the people in your office a heads-up. I have a team heading in there now, too."

Grace stepped aside at a tap on the door. Over Harold Dennis's increasingly voluble protests, she twisted the handle and allowed a group of sheriff's deputies to enter the room.

Matthew watched them pass without moving. "I'll call, but I'm not stepping out."

He called his assistant, Tracy.

"Matthew? What's happening? Nate's in a hell of a mood."

"Hey, listen, I can't talk long," he said to his assistant. "Some stuff is about to go down with Nate. I can't get into it now. I need you to stay calm and make sure everyone else does, too. I'll be there as soon as I can."

He ended the call to preempt the barrage of questions he knew would be forthcoming. As Grace directed the deputies to each of the persons they'd identified as party guests, he speed-dialed his boss.

"What the hell is going on?" Nate snapped. "Where are you?"

"I'm at the offices of Powers, Powers & Walton," he replied calmly.

"Why? We've talked about this. Nothing good can come of—"

"I'm watching your friend Trey Powers get cuffed as we speak," Matthew said, cutting him off. "They're also taking guys named Joshua Potter and Chet Barrow, as well as a Ms. Taylor Greene into custody for questioning."

"On what grounds?" Nate demanded. Matthew heard the echo of a hard rap on a door and held his breath.

Nate place a finger over the microphone to muffle the sound, but his voice still came through clear enough when he called out, "Come back later. I'm busy."

"I don't think they'll come back later, Nate," Matthew said quietly.

Through the phone he could hear a louder knock and an officious voice call out, "Nathaniel Able?"

Nate came back on the line. "What the hell is this, Murray? What's happening here?"

"I'm afraid Taylor Greene has placed you at the same party she was attending the evening Mallory went missing," he explained. "The party at the Powerses' lake house."

"She's lying," Nate responded without hesitation.

"Unfortunately for you, she's not. I've seen photographs of the two of you together. Come on, Nate, you know the internet is forever. How could you have been so foolish?"

The minute the question escaped him, Matthew wondered if he was asking his boss how he'd been foolish enough to get caught, or foolish enough to put himself in the situation to start. Either way, it didn't matter. Nate's career as a prosecutor and his dreams of political glory were likely over.

Or not. It seemed politicians were able to get away with far more these days. Perhaps the cover-up of Mallory's death would end up being something Nate would have to spin, but it was possible the scandal wouldn't keep him from winning future elections. Particularly not if his wife stayed by his side.

And if he stayed on the right side of Tyrone Powers.

"Go with them quietly. Answer what questions you can and be sure to give Susan some warning."

"I swear, if you've done anything to jeopardize my—"

"I haven't done anything other than try to find out what happened to my sister. You remember my sister now, don't you, Nate? She's the one you and your buddies left floating alone in the dark on Table Rock Lake."

"I have no idea what you're talking about," Nate said stiffly.

Matthew swallowed hard. All around him, deputies were snapping handcuffs and running through the litany of arrest. From the head of the table, Harold Dennis barked out the names of other attorneys in the room, assigning one to each of the detainees.

He heard the deputy on the other end of the line say to Nate, "I'm going to need you to end your call and come with me, sir."

Three short beeps marked the disconnection. Matthew lowered the phone and stepped to the side, allowing one of the deputies to lead a bewildered-looking Joshua Potter from the room. He watched as the deputy leading Barrow followed, the younger man grumbling under his breath about how they were all making a big, big mistake. Grace stepped in beside him while Taylor Greene was led out the door; her eyes were downcast, but her frustrated sobs had dried to hiccups.

"You okay?" she asked in a low voice as two more attorneys scurried out of the room.

"Yeah."

Matthew's focus shifted to Trey Powers, who stood conferring with his father and lawyers. The deputy had cuffed his hands in front of him but kept a loose hold on the crook of his arm. Matthew noticed how he'd subtly turned away from their hissed whispers. Even under arrest, the Powers men received special treatment.

"You'd better head to your office while I deal with all this. It's going to be a circus over there."

Matthew nodded. "You're probably right."

"I'm going to have to get the Carroll County prosecutor filled in, but I'll touch base with you as soon as I get a minute."

"I doubt any of them talk from here on out."

Grace gave him a half smile. "I think Taylor will. I believe the young woman may actually have one of those...what do you call it? A moral compass?"

"I wouldn't know," Matthew replied, deadpan.

"Oh, right, you're one of them, too."

"I am not one of them," he shot back immediately.

Grace gave his arm a reassuring pat. "No. No, you're not."

Stepping forward, she turned her attention to the group on the other side of the room. Tyrone and Trey seemed to be stalling while Harold Dennis conferred with Michelle Fraser.

"Mr. Powers?" Grace prompted. When they deigned to turn her way, she raised both eyebrows and smirked at the powerful trio. "I promise y'all will have hours to play catch-up, but you're holding me and Deputy, uh..." She tilted her head, trying to read the name pinned to the officer's uniform.

"Smith," he supplied for her.

"You're keeping Deputy Smith from his other duties, and I'm tired of waiting for you. Let's move it out."

With the brusque order, Grace unleashed a smile so triumphant, Matthew felt his chest tighten even as Tyrone Powers flushed nearly violet.

At last, Trey started to move to the door with Michelle Fraser close on his heels, but Tyrone Powers halted them with an abrupt "Stop!" With a fiery glare at Grace, he unbuttoned the jacket of his exquisitely tailored suit. "Hold out your arms," he instructed his son.

Trey did as he was told, but in doing so, the sleeves of his own suit jacket rode up.

Recognition shot through Matthew like a lightning bolt when he spotted the expensive watch on the man's wrist. Grace must have seen it, too, because she straightened to her full height as the older man draped his folded jacket over his son's wrists to conceal the cuffs.

Grace gave Matthew a speaking glance before she fell into step behind Trey and the deputy. "I like your cuff links," she said in a voice loud enough to carry back to him. "And they match your watch. Such a pretty blue. Are they white gold or platinum?"

Matthew had to stifle a chuckle as he followed the two older lawyers out of the conference room and toward the exterior doors. Harold Dennis held one of the glass panel doors open for them to pass through, but Tyrone hung back.

Matthew could only assume it was because he wanted to put distance between Grace and themselves as he whispered, "This was not your brightest hour, Murray. When we're through with you, no one will elect you dogcatcher."

Meeting the other man's steely gaze, Matthew simply shrugged. "I guess it's a good thing I'm not running for dogcatcher."

While Grace and the others headed for the parking area, Matthew took off at a brisk pace in the opposite direction. His gaze fixed straight ahead, he power walked down Central toward the courthouse and the county offices. Cutting through to one of the back entrances, he passed the spot where he'd backed into Judge Walton's car a lifetime ago.

He nodded to the sheriff's deputy on security duty, showed his ID and emptied his pockets into a tray to be clear for the metal detector. Once he'd collected his belongings, he turned down the main corridor and started off in a trot. He reached the prosecuting attorney's offices just as Nate was being escorted into the hall wearing a set of cuffs.

Stripping off his own jacket, Matthew threw it over the shiny silver bracelets his boss wore.

"Yeah, thanks a lot," Nate said derisively.

"We're not even going to get into who did what to whom," Matthew said in a low voice. "My advice to you is to cooperate. Help them build this case. You know what Powers did was wrong. You know you're all accessories after the fact regardless. Cut whatever deal you need to cut and save what's left of your life. Otherwise, I will do everything I can to make sure your career is buried along with my sister. You got me?"

Nate sneered as he reared back. "Thanks for your unsolicited advice, Counselor."

"Take it or leave it," Matthew called after him as the deputies led him away. "Free of charge and everything. Bet you Powers won't say the same thing."

When he turned back to the open door, he found every pair of eyes in the office trained on him. Sparing one last glance at Nate's back, Matthew stepped into the office and did his best to make order out of chaos.

Chapter Eighteen

Though she expected the knock at her door, Grace still jumped when it came. The weeks following the arrests of the people involved with Mallory Murray's disappearance and death had been maddening. As Matthew predicted, most of the Powers team clammed up. They could barely get single-word answers out of any of them without another attorney vetting the question and approving their answer or nonanswer.

Thankfully, Nate Able had decided to give the press a couple of sound bites on the courthouse steps upon his release on bond. He'd stated he had not witnessed any part of Ms. Murray's misadventure, claimed he'd never believed there was anything to cover up because he didn't know anything had happened, but worst of all, he'd categorically denied the affair he was accused of having with one of the attorneys at PP&W.

The problems for Nate compounded when his wife, Susan, refused to return from Florida and take her place by his side. Instead, she told the press she had been aware of her husband's infidelity and had hired an investigator to follow him to gather proof in the week she was gone. Her investigator was able to produce photos taken the morning after the party. The incriminating photographs showed the Benton County prosecuting attorney behind the wheel of a gray compact car matching the description of the deceased's vehicle.

Within minutes of his second arrest, the county board called for Nate's resignation. Matthew had been appointed acting prosecuting attorney within the day. It was all such a whirlwind he and Grace had barely had a minute to exchange text messages and voice mails updating one another on what was happening on their end.

After a week of spending a good chunk of their waking hours together, Grace found herself missing him. Not only his insights and the company, but his presence. Now he stood outside the open door to her hotel room waiting to be invited in. Her heart started to beat faster as she drank in the sight of him. He was dressed in chinos and a short-sleeved button-down. Even his casual clothes fit his long, lean body like a glove.

"Hey," she said, stepping back to allow him entry. "What a crazy couple of weeks, huh?"

"An understatement." He looked her up and down, a smile tugging at his lips. "You look, uh—" he paused for a beat "—nice."

Color raced to her cheeks. At first, she wasn't sure if he was holding back or simply being polite, but his smile was warm and appreciative.

"You didn't have to dress up," he said, but everything about his demeanor told her he was glad she had.

When he'd asked her to come with him to the cemetery where Mallory's ashes would be placed beside their parents', she'd realized she didn't have anything appropriate to wear. Everything she owned was cop wear, and in this instance, she wanted him to see her as more than a detective. So she'd made a quick trip to the mall, where she bought a casual but pretty dress and sandals her sister approved via video chat.

"Thanks for your help with the jurisdictional mess," he said sincerely.

"It was the least I could do," she replied, trying to sound offhand but unable to control her skittering heartbeat.

With the backing of the state police, Grace was able to get the junior Benton County attorney Matthew had assigned to the case, the Carroll County PA and officials from the federal government to agree on referring the case to one of the circuit courts in central Arkansas. Hopefully, the move would be enough to mitigate some of the family's influence on the court system.

His gaze traveled around the sitting area. She'd packed up most of her gear already. By evening, she'd be back in her apartment in Fort Smith, and the following week she'd be at her desk again, catching the missing-persons cases no one else wanted to handle.

"Looks like you're about ready to clear out."

"I got most of it gathered last night," she answered, trying to sound indifferent.

He gave a sigh and a tired smile. "I guess we should go do this."

Grace nodded, then grabbed her purse and keys from the breakfast bar.

Matthew pulled his own key ring from his pocket and jangled it. "I'm driving this time."

"I don't know… Is it safe to ride with the mysterious bumper smasher?" she teased, pulling the door shut behind her.

"Yeah, now you're making me wish it was some kind of jacked-up 4x4," he complained good-naturedly.

He held the car door for her as she slid into the sporty SUV parked beside her decidedly more clunky-looking state vehicle.

Neither of them spoke as they left the parking area and headed northeast on Highway 62. The moment they were outside the city limits, he glanced over at her. "It means a lot to me, you coming along today. I didn't want to do a whole service and everything."

"I understand."

"They threw a party in Mallory's honor at Stubby's last weekend."

"Did you go?"

He shook his head. "Nah. Never was my scene, and I figured me being there would make people feel like they had to behave in front of the bereaved brother."

She nodded. "Kelli Simon told me you cleared Mallory's things out of the apartment."

He nodded. "There wasn't much to keep. I donated most of her clothes and stuff."

"Nice," she said approvingly.

The miles flew by, and they slipped into the same easy silence they'd had since the start. As they passed Stubby's Bar & Grill, the back of her neck prickled, but Grace chalked the sensation up to residual excitement at closing the case.

The scene at the modest cemetery east of Garfield might have looked sad to anyone passing by, but somehow it seemed right for Matthew and Mallory. Grace hung back, standing close to the man who'd opened the small grave while Matthew knelt beside a headstone carved with only the family name.

She bowed her head as he spoke.

"I'm sorry, Mal. Sorry we weren't closer. Sorry I wasn't a better brother. Sorry this happened to you." He paused to take a shuddering breath. "I know this guy is slippery, but I promise you, we will go after him with everything we have. Trey Powers will pay for what he did to you."

Grace sighed. At the moment, the biggest charge they could nail Powers with was leaving the scene, but she knew deep in her bones Matthew was right. They would find the key. Trey Powers would not get off on a technicality or buy his way out of this mess with his family's money.

After Matthew had spoken his piece and his sister was laid to rest, he and Grace returned to the car. The moment they were back on the highway, he shot her an uneasy glance. "I don't know if I could possibly come up with a more inappropriate time and place to say what I want to say to you, but if I've learned anything from Mallory's death, it's that I have to say it anyway."

"Okay," she replied, curiosity piqued.

"I like you, Grace. Despite the circumstances, I liked being with you. And I would like to see more of you." He cast another sidelong glance in her direction. "Not in a professional capacity."

Once again, her heart began to pound. "I, uh, yeah. I feel the same way, but I didn't want to say something because—" she circled a hand, hoping to encompass all the circumstances under which they met "—everything."

"Fort Smith isn't far," he ventured.

"Nope. It's an easy drive up 49."

He let off the gas as soon as they hit a straight stretch and turned to her. "Would you have dinner with me one night? We can meet in the middle if you want."

She smirked as she envisioned the rural stretch of highway between the cities of Fort Smith and Fayetteville. "I think they do two-for-one corn dogs at the gas station in West Fork."

The suggestion earned her a grin. "Okay, I'll come to you."

"Either way," she said agreeably.

They drove in contented quiet for a minute. When Matthew reached over and touched the back of her hand, she turned it palm up. He laced his fingers through hers.

"You're not going to give me a ticket for not having both hands on the wheel, are you?"

"I can be bribed."

"Oh, yeah?" He gave her fingers a squeeze. "With what?"

She jerked her chin toward the squat cinder-block building they approached. "Buy me a Stubby's burger? I hear they're the best around."

Without releasing her hand, he signaled his intention to turn into the crumbling asphalt lot.

Inside the dimly lit bar, they waved hello to Steve.

"You're late for the party," he informed them.

"How was it?" Grace asked as Matthew pointed to a table.

"It was a doozy," their resident day drinker called from his seat at the end of the bar.

"Can we get two burgers?" Matthew asked, holding up two fingers.

"Coming up," Steve replied.

"Water?" he asked Grace.

"Please." She hooked a thumb over her shoulder. "I'm going to the ladies'."

Matthew nodded, and she walked away. A part of her wanted to do a giddy dance. He wanted to see her again.

Slipping into the dank ladies' room, she locked the door behind her and pulled her phone from her bag. Thumbs flying, she texted her sister.

He asked me out!

While she waited to see if the dots indicating an incoming message appeared, she glanced up and caught sight of an ancient metal vending machine attached to the wall. One side purported to sell feminine products and the other condoms.

She focused on her phone again. No message from her sister came through, but the creeping sensation along the back of her neck had returned. She spun in a slow circle. Out of the corner of her eye, she noticed that the door to the vending machine wasn't properly secured.

There were no scratches to indicate someone had tried to pry it open, but a shiver traveled down her spine. Dropping her phone back into her bag, Grace reached for the corner of the cabinet and pulled.

A shower of paper-wrapped tampons and condom

squares spilled out at her feet. As did a zip-top bag holding a white wand with a blue cap and a plastic card.

Grace squatted to make a closer inspection. Using the hem of her dress, she picked up one corner of the bag. The white stick showed a clear plus sign in the window. Mallory Murray beamed back at her from an Arkansas driver's license.

"There you are," Grace whispered as she inspected the bag's contents to be certain she wasn't imagining her good fortune.

She wasn't.

It wasn't quite the gotcha she needed to nail Trey Powers for murder, but the fact Mallory had hidden these items might help prove she was concerned about his reaction to the news of his impending fatherhood.

Releasing the bag, she reached for her phone again. Ignoring the rapid-fire texts from her sister about what she'd wear and where they'd go, Grace shot several photos of the bag, its contents, the wrapped tampons and condoms, and finally the machine itself.

Covering the bag in a paper towel to protect it, she stepped out into the barroom and walked up to Steve at the bar. "I'm sorry," she murmured, "I'm going to need to cordon off your ladies' room. Would you please call the county sheriff to come out?"

"What is it?" Matthew asked, rising from the nearby table where he sat with their sweating drinks.

"I found test number two and Mallory's driver's license," she informed him. "This isn't over."

She held up her phone to show him the photos she'd snapped. He swallowed hard, still looking at the screen as another message from Faith came through.

Take a picture of him. I need a visual. Oh, and whatever you do, don't let Hottie McMurray see you in
your cop suit.

"Too late," he whispered, looking down at her with
such blatant admiration her breath tangled in her throat.
"Tell her I've seen you in your cop suit, Grace, and it
was a beautiful sight to behold."

"We'll get him, Matthew. Somehow, someway, we'll
make sure this sticks."

Looking straight into her eyes, he lowered his head
until his lips were mere millimeters from hers. "Yes.
We will."

His kiss was soft. Lingering. Filled with promise.

"Have I told you how glad I am we're on the same
side?"

"No, but I am, too," she whispered. "I'd hate to have
to take you down."

* * * * *

COMING NEXT MONTH FROM

ⓗ HARLEQUIN

INTRIGUE

#2145 HER BRAND OF JUSTICE
A Colt Brothers Investigation • by B.J. Daniels

Ansley Brookshire's quest to uncover the truth about her adoption leads her to Lonesome, Montana—and into the arms cowboy Buck Crawford. But someone doesn't want the truth to come out...and will do *anything* to halt Ansley and Buck's search. Even kill.

#2146 TRAPPED IN TEXAS
The Cowboys of Cider Creek • by Barb Han

With a deadly stalker closing in, rising country star Raelynn Simmons needs to stay off the stage—and off the grid. Agent Sean Hayes accepts one last mission to keep her safe from danger. But with flying bullets putting them in close proximity, who will keep Sean's heart safe from Raelynn?

#2147 DEAD AGAIN
Defenders of Battle Mountain • by Nichole Severn

Macie Barclay never stopped searching for her best friend's murderer...until a dead body and a new lead reunites her with her ex, Detective Riggs Karig. Riggs knows he and Macie are playing with fire. Especially when she becomes the killer's next target...

#2148 WYOMING MOUNTAIN MURDER
Cowboy State Lawmen • by Juno Rushdan

Charlie Sharp knows how to defend herself. But when a client goes missing—presumed dead—she must rely on Detective Brian Bradshaw to uncover the truth. As they dig for clues and discover more dead bodies, all linked to police corruption, can they learn to trust each other to survive?

#2149 OZARKS DOUBLE HOMICIDE
Arkansas Special Agents • by Maggie Wells

A grisly double homicide threatens Michelle Fraser's yearslong undercover assignment. But the biggest threat to the FBI agent is Lieutenant Ethan Scott. He knows the seemingly innocent attorney is hiding something. But when they untangle a political money laundering conspiracy, how far will he go to keep Michelle's secrets?

#2150 DANGER IN THE NEVADA DESERT
by Denise N. Wheatley

Nevada's numeric serial killer is on a rampage—and his crimes are getting personal. When Sergeant Charlotte Bowman teams up with Detective Miles Love to capture the deranged murderer before another life is lost, they must fight grueling, deadly circumstances...and their undeniable attraction.

YOU CAN FIND MORE INFORMATION ON UPCOMING HARLEQUIN TITLES, FREE EXCERPTS AND MORE AT HARLEQUIN.COM.

HICNM0423

HARLEQUIN
PLUS

Try the best multimedia subscription service for romance readers like you!

Read, Watch and Play.

Experience the easiest way to get the romance content you crave.

Start your **FREE TRIAL** at
<u>www.harlequinplus.com/freetrial</u>.